Eternal Series

Eternal Echoes

Book One

By:

Autumn Marie

Chapter One
The Shadow Man

Since as far back as I can recall, I have been constantly on the move. It feels like an eternity has passed since I first started running. Yet, no matter how fast or how far I sprinted, the shadowy figure always managed to track me down. His presence was an ever-present force, always looming over me. He seemed to anticipate my every move, leading me into traps and dead ends that left me scrambling in desperation.

My heart raced with fear, my body was drenched in sweat as I paused to catch my breath. Surveying my surroundings, I meticulously examined every detail of the labyrinth I found myself in. The towering city buildings cast a foreboding shadow, their neglected and dilapidated structures adding to the eerie atmosphere.

As I stood there, feeling the weight of the shadow man's gaze upon me, I knew that I had to find a way out of this maze before it was too late.

The scene before me resembled something out of an apocalyptic movie. Debris littered the city streets, and there was a noticeable absence of plant life. Abandoned vehicles obstructed the roads, with broken windshields and dents making them seem like obstacles waiting to be navigated. Some cars lay on their sides as if a giant toddler had knocked them over in a fit of rage. A few streetlamps flickered weakly, casting a dim glow that barely illuminated my surroundings.

Despite the desolate landscape, I couldn't shake the feeling of being watched. My shadowy companion lurked in the darkness, his presence felt everywhere.

With trepidation, I continued walking until I reached an intersection. Uncertain of which way to go, I scanned each street but couldn't see far enough to determine if any of them led to dead ends.

Right. I'll take a right.

After what felt like an eternity of walking, a glimmer of light caught my eye in the distance. Intrigued, I quickened my pace towards the source of the illumination. To my surprise, the light emanated from a brightly colored car engulfed in flames.

I hesitated, a sense of unease creeping over me. Could this be some sort of trap? The burning vehicle stood alone on the desolate road, intensifying my suspicions.

My heart raced as I cautiously approached the fiery spectacle. The pounding of my heart reverberated in my ears, drowning out all other sounds. A peculiar noise emanated from the car, growing louder as I drew nearer. It resembled the frantic gasps of someone in the throes of a panic attack.

Kneeling, I peered inside the vehicle, only to find it empty, leaving me with more questions than answers.

So, where was the noise coming from??

Once I regained my footing, I approached the rear of the vehicle and discovered a figure curled up in the fetal position. The individual's posture made it difficult to discern their gender. Their hands shielded their face as they emitted a chilling sound while trembling.

A lump formed in my throat, hindering my ability to speak. My voice quivered as I asked, "Are you okay?"

The figure remained silent and did not acknowledge my presence. *Had I spoken too softly?*

I cleared my throat and tried again, "Excuse me... Do you need help?"

Once again, my presence went unnoticed.

"Please, allow me to help you," I offered, extending my hand towards the figure. Just as my fingers were about to touch their shoulder, the being abruptly turned to face me. Startled, I recoiled and let out a horrified scream. Its face... there wasn't one.

Devoid of eyes, nose, ears, or mouth, the creature stood before me, a sight too terrifying to put into words.

I took a few steps back as the being rose to its feet, emitting a deafening sound. It began to move towards me slowly, its hand outstretched in my direction.

I didn't know what to make of the terrifying situation. So I did the only thing that made sense. I ran.

As I sprinted back in the direction I had come from, I glanced over my shoulder to witness the shadows enveloping the figure behind me.

A wave of relief washed over me, but I was aware that it would be short-lived.

And I was right. While fleeing, the streetlights that had been guiding my path suddenly extinguished, leaving me in complete darkness. Panic set in as I realized I could potentially come face-to-face with my Shadow Man.

How do I get out of here?? I thought to myself. *If there's no way out... Then maybe I need to find a safe place to hide.*

There has to be a way out of here.

As I strolled past the row of deserted buildings, a flicker of light caught my attention. The sudden illumination was a peculiar sight, as these buildings had always remained shrouded in darkness before. Intrigued, I approached the window from which the light emanated, hoping to catch a glimpse of what lay inside.

To my astonishment, I saw my best friend Sara standing in the room. Her tear-streaked face bore a look of sheer terror and despair. Without a moment's hesitation, I called out her name and began frantically pounding on the window, desperate to reach her.

She remained unresponsive to my calls and the banging on the window. Determined to get her attention, I knocked on the window even louder, disregarding the possibility of breaking the glass, all the while calling out her name with increasing volume. Despite my efforts, she continued to ignore me.

Then, suddenly, Sara jumped. I believed that I had finally caught her attention and felt a wave of relief wash over me that she had finally reacted. However, I soon realized that my assumption was far from the truth...

She was startled when the door to the room burst open with an incredible amount of force. My friend was standing in the middle of the room, slowly retreating from the entrance, her eyes fixed on whatever or whoever was in front of her. As she dropped to her knees, I could hear her pleading with some unseen entity, begging it to release her.

A crimson light began to emanate from the room, gradually enveloping everything. I tried to keep my gaze on Sara, but she disappeared into the light. Just when I thought I couldn't bear the intense red glow any longer, it slowly dimmed. That's when I saw her lifeless body sprawled on the floor.

"Sara!" I cried out, pounding on the window with increasing intensity.

A deep, sinister laugh echoed through the room.

Tears streamed down my face as the menacing laughter taunted me, enveloping the scene in darkness like the final act of a tragic play. I stared into the pitch-black room, paralyzed with fear and unable to move or think.

As the ominous laughter faded, a chilling breath brushed against the back of my neck. I stood frozen as a cold hand, with unusually long fingers, gripped my right wrist. Fear consumed me, causing my heart to falter and my breath to escape me. Suddenly, I was forcefully turned around to come face to face with the Shadow Man.

This imposing figure towered over my 5-foot 2-inch frame by at least two to three feet. His face was concealed by a black hooded cloak, but his hands, pale and almost gray, were visible. His long, spindly fingers seemed out of proportion with the rest of his body.

"Well, well..." his deep, booming voice rumbled. "It seems the cat has finally caught the mouse."

I remained frozen, unable to find my words.

"Aww, what's the matter Ember?" The shadow man chuckled.

"What seems to be troubling you, Ember?" The shadow man chuckled.

I was caught off guard by the familiarity with which he addressed me. This nightmare was unlike anything I had ever experienced before, especially coming face to face with the shadow man.

How does he know my name?

"I know all about you, Ember," his voice echoed as if he could read my mind. "I know more about you than you know about yourself," he continued with a hint of amusement in his tone.

His words lingered in the air, leaving me with a sense of dread.

I looked up into the darkness that obscured his face, rendered speechless. My mind raced to the figure that had barged in before my friend fell to the ground, unmoving.

The man smirked as he uttered, "Your friend is insignificant. She was weak and inconsequential." A chilling laugh slipped from his mouth. "I have more pressing matters to discuss with you. That girl you consider a *friend* would only hinder us."

His words ignited a fire within me. "Don't talk of my friend that way! Who the hell do you think you are?"

He laughed in amusement. "Well, look who suddenly grew a backbone!"

I fixed my gaze on him, my voice trembling with anger as I spoke, "You have no right to determine who lives and who dies in this world!" However, I found myself silently questioning his motives. He stood before me, a living embodiment of Death, devoid of the scythe.

The imposing figure let out another chuckle. Despite his eerie demeanor, he seemed to find amusement in our confrontation. "Dear Ember," he began, his words sending a chill down my spine, "I am far more sinister than Death."

I was taken aback by the revelation. "How do you know what I'm thinking?" I asked in disbelief.

As soon as the words left my mouth, the entity's demeanor changed from amusement to frustration as he turned away from me. "This is why I cannot stand humans.." He let out a disapproving sigh. "Everything, all of the potential that you people hold is completely wasted upon your species!"

"If you hate our kind so much then why am I here? Why do you keep following me? Why do you keep bringing me to this nightmarish realm time and time again?"

As the figure turned to me once more, he began, "Because you hold great value to me."

This guy is crazy…

"Do NOT call me crazy!" he bellowed. "Centuries! Centuries I have wasted upon you, watching you grow, rediscovering your secrets, waiting for you to gain enough strength to carry out my plans..." He trailed off.

"What do you mean by centuries?" I replied skeptically. "And what makes you so sure that I would help you?"

He chuckled. "Do not ever think you are capable of deceiving me, Ember. I always know where you are, what you're thinking, what breaks you, and what makes you give in. I am aware of all your failures, even the ones you have long forgotten." He moved closer. "So do not even dare to think you are smart enough to mislead me."

I became cocky. "Obviously, if I am the only person who can help you, then when I say no, I mean it when I say I will not help you. You can imprison me. You can torture me. But you cannot kill me."

Another uncontrollable laugh erupted from the figure. "Not kill you? I honestly couldn't care less whether you live or die. It's merely an inconvenience when you die. However, you always turn back up, making it quite easy to track you down."

"I always turn back up?" I replied inquisitively. "What are you talking about?"

The cloaked man let out a long, frustrated sigh before turning away in exasperation. As he grumbled under his breath, I saw an opportunity to escape. I had spent most of my life running from him, so why not a little more?

Suddenly, his voice rang out, "You cannot run from me, Ember."

Before I could react, I felt his icy grip around my throat. Despite my efforts to leave him behind, I had only managed to run straight into his clutches. Gasping for air, I struggled as his hold tightened and he pushed me against a nearby building. "Found you."

Desperately, I grabbed at his wrist and managed to croak out, "Who are you?"

My name is Lucien, and you are coming with me," his voice was stern. "You are mine."

"No!" I croaked, unable to speak any further. Rage gripped me at his possessiveness.

He brought his head closer to mine, but I still couldn't see any details of his face. "Why do you say no, my dear? Don't you want to come with me?"

Panic overwhelmed my senses. I couldn't breathe, I couldn't speak. I was convinced that at that moment, I would die.

"You humans are quite entertaining when you are inches away from death," he said. "The way you squirm, the way your minds race, unable to keep a clear thought in your little heads."

I was filled with disgust as he disapprovingly stated, "Pathetic," before dropping me to my knees.

"My people can tear through yours like tissue paper." His voice agitated. "How can someone like you be placed in a world like this? So filthy and dishonorable. No pride, no strength--only weakness and beggary."

I struggled to focus on his speech, my coughing interrupting every inhale. Finally catching my breath, I blurted out, "Why do you speak as if you're so superior? What are you, some kind of demon?"

The comparison to a demon seemed to amuse Lucien, prompting him to chuckle. "My dear Ember, I am far worse than what you humans perceive as a demon."

A wave of anxiety swept over me, my instincts confirming the truth in his words. Nausea crept in as he laughed at my vulnerability, mocking my very existence.

"You fail to recognize the mysteries that surround you. Many are convinced that humans are the sole inhabitants of the universe, attributing unusual events to ghosts, ghouls, or demons. However, I exist in a realm parallel to yours, hidden in plain sight. A place you have unknowingly crossed paths with countless times and will inevitably encounter again. Your presence in my world will grant me increased power and strength, abilities beyond imagination that will inspire envy in all who witness them." Lucien delivered his speech with unwavering confidence, but I had tuned out by then.

I was still trying to process the bombshell he had just dropped. What was he talking about? How could I possibly have the ability to do what he was asking of me? I couldn't wrap my head around it. He called me a weak human, yet claimed I possessed some extraordinary power. It was a conflicting thought - on the one hand, I was curious to understand how I could have such abilities, but on the other hand, I feared becoming a mere puppet if I did.

Interrupting his speech, I asked, "What do you mean I exist in a realm parallel to yours? Are you talking about another dimension?"

Lucien's cloaked head turned sharply in my direction. "Have you ever wondered why you are so different from everyone else?"

I remained silent in response to his question. Naturally, I had always questioned how and why I possessed the ability to do things deemed impossible.

As Lucien seemed poised to launch into yet another lengthy monologue, a streetlight to our left began to flicker. The sudden movement of light drew our gaze in that direction, where we noticed a figure standing beneath it. Judging by the figure's height and build, it was clear that the individual was male.

"Let her go!" The stranger demanded, his voice exuding unwavering confidence.

Lucien instantly grew angry at the intruder's presence. "What are you doing here?" He hissed.

I found myself wondering about the connection between the two, as it was clear that this was not their initial encounter.

As the enigmatic man approached, his eyes came into view. They were a mesmerizing shade of green, accented by a deep yellow hue around his pupils. His gaze intensified as he sternly commanded, "I said, let her go, NOW." The stranger's voice resonated with authority and determination.

As he approached, a sense of security washed over me. It was as if I could finally let my guard down in his presence. There was something about him that exuded trustworthiness, despite the fact that I didn't know him at all. A strange connection seemed to exist between us, one that defied explanation. It felt as though an invisible force was drawing us closer together, intensifying as he neared.

I found myself gazing at him, transfixed like a deer in headlights. His presence was mesmerizing, and I couldn't resist taking a step towards him. However, my actions seemed to anger Lucien, who forcefully pushed me back against the building, causing my head to collide with the wall with a jolt.

Lucien made a swift escape, with the enigmatic man hot on his heels, leaving me to collapse to my knees. I clutched my head, overwhelmed by an indescribable pain that pulsed through my forehead with each heartbeat. The rhythmic thumping of my heart reverberated in my ears, intensifying the agony.

Suddenly, a hand rested on my shoulder, jolting me from my daze. Startled, I remained still, focusing solely on the excruciating pain that consumed me, blocking out everything else around me.

"Are you alright?" The handsome man asked, his voice filled with concern.

"My head is killing me, but I'll be fine," I replied, looking up at him. My heart skipped a beat as I stared into his beautiful, worry-filled eyes.

"You have a pretty good-sized bump on your head already."

A wave of embarrassment washed over me as I hurriedly composed myself. The man before me flashed a charming smile, revealing his impeccably straight, white teeth.

"Thank you for chasing Lucien away," I expressed my gratitude. A brief silence followed as he gazed intently into my eyes, causing my cheeks to flush once more. Clearing my throat, I asked, "Who are you?"

"Aiden."

"I'm Ember."

He laughed. "I know who you are."

"How does everyone here know who I am?" I questioned, feeling perplexed and aggravated.

"This is not the time or place to answer that, my love," Aiden replied, casting a glance at the shadows that enveloped us. He extended his hand to help me up.

Typically, being called "my love" by someone would instantly enrage me. However, inexplicably, it did not bother me when Aiden said it.

When our skin made contact, a powerful, electrifying sensation surged through my body. It was a thrilling feeling that I didn't want to end. Just as I was about to ask about this sensation, Aiden began to speak.

"You are still as beautiful as ever," he said, causing my heart to falter as he gently caressed my cheek and tucked a loose strand of hair behind my ear.

I found myself speechless as Aiden continued to stroke my cheek and gaze deeply into my eyes. I couldn't help but wonder why his touch sent shivers down my spine and left me yearning for more. Why did my mind feel like it was in a fog whenever he was near?

Aiden continued smiling at me.

"Why do you call me 'love'?" I finally managed to say after staring at him for a long time. It wasn't exactly the question I had intended to ask, but it was the one that slipped out.

His smile persisted as he replied, "You will find out soon enough." He paused, then added, "When I find you."

His words left me feeling perplexed, and I continued to stare at him, feeling like a lovesick preteen.

Aiden began to lean his head towards mine as if he were about to kiss me. With each inch he closed the distance between us, my heart pounded in my chest. A rush of heat flooded my face and my breath hitched in my throat, while butterflies danced wildly in my stomach. I held my breath in anticipation as his lips hovered just inches from mine...

When I woke up.

Chapter Two

Acquaintance

Why do I always wake up at the best part?.. He was going to kiss me! I wondered as I glanced over at my alarm clock. Letting out a frustrated groan, I noticed the glaring 4 a.m. displayed on the clock. Sleep seemed to evade me as my mind raced with thoughts. Tossing and turning in bed, I struggled to find a comfortable position. Frustrated, I threw off the blankets in annoyance and sat up, only to be met with a sharp pain that shot through my head, causing me to fall back onto my pillow.

After the pain had subsided to a more bearable level, I made my way to the bathroom. My long brunette hair was a tangled mess from sleep, so I quickly brushed it and styled it into a side braid. Looking at my reflection in the mirror, I stared into my bright blue eyes, trying to calm myself. I attempted to clear my mind of any thoughts, but the silence of the house only allowed my mind to drift back to the nightmare that had plagued my sleep.

I had to get out of here. I needed to go for a walk to clear my thoughts.

After brushing my teeth, I quickly got dressed and made sure to grab my cell phone and earbuds. The hallway was shrouded in darkness as I navigated my way through the house, careful not to disturb my parents who were still fast asleep. My father's loud snores echoed through the house, a comforting reminder that they were safe and sound.

I tiptoed towards the front door, not wanting to wake my parents. They had already endured so much with my recurring nightmares, and I didn't want to burden them with something they couldn't control or fix.

The same terrifying dream had haunted me since I was just four years old, growing more frequent and intense as the years passed. My parents, always worried about my night terrors, had taken me to countless doctors in search of a solution, but nothing seemed to help. I was repeatedly assured that it was just a phase I would eventually outgrow.

As a result, I stopped sharing my nightmares with others and keeping them to myself. Occasionally, the fear would be so overwhelming that I would wake up screaming in terror, a stark reminder of the ongoing battle I faced every night.

As I stepped outside, the frigid winter breeze pierced through me like icy daggers. It was the heart of January, prompting me to layer up with multiple coats and my trusty scarf. Walking alone in the serene early morning, each step I took was met with a loud crunch as the snow beneath me protested.

The neighborhood was transformed into a winter wonderland, with a thick blanket of snow covering everything in sight. Front lawns were adorned with charming snowmen crafted by the neighborhood children. The air still carried a hint of the festive energy from Christmas, lingering like a sweet memory.

As I strolled through the quiet streets, it was evident that everyone was still nestled snugly in their warm beds, lost in peaceful dreams. The moon and stars were obscured by heavy clouds looming overhead, casting a shadow over the landscape. The only source of light came from the streetlamps that stood sentinel along the sidewalk, guiding my way through the tranquil winter morning.

As I walked along, the city skyline gradually came into view, prompting me to reach for my phone and tune into some music.

I am aware that it is not wise to be oblivious to one's surroundings in the city. However, given the scarcity of people out and about at this early hour, I saw no harm in indulging myself. Another reason I sought solace in music was to drown out the noise of the world around me. People's thoughts can be overwhelmingly intrusive. Not only did I have to contend with recurring nightmares that haunted my sleep, but I also bore the burden of being able to hear the thoughts of those around me.

Sara always insisted that I was blessed to possess such a gift, but let me assure you, it felt more like a curse. While many might view this ability as advantageous in some way, for me, it was pure torment.

The most effective method I discovered for combating intrusive thoughts was by listening to music at a high volume. While it didn't completely silence everyone's internal monologue, it did help to reduce it to a mere background noise.

I strolled to the park and settled onto a bench to watch the sunrise. As time passed, the park became more bustling with people rushing to grab breakfast and coffee before heading to work. I observed them without any particular thoughts, attempting to push aside the strange feeling that had come over me. After the sun had fully risen, I decided to wander aimlessly until I either grew tired or felt ready to return home.

Watching others head off to work always stirred up a twinge of envy within me. Despite my best efforts over the years, I struggled to maintain steady employment due to my unique telepathic ability. I couldn't simply drown out the world with earbuds while on the job. The thoughts of others could be overwhelming, often leaving me feeling uneasy. I encountered bosses with unsavory intentions and coworkers with equally distasteful thoughts. The workplace was rife with jealousy, betrayal, and insincerity, reminiscent of high school drama.

It was around 8 a.m. when I made the decision to leave the park, still lost in my music. The city streets were bustling with people going about their daily routines. As I navigated through the crowded sidewalks and streets, I instinctively tuned out the thoughts of those around me. That is until I stumbled upon a building that had previously gone unnoticed.

For the past six years, I have traversed these streets without ever laying eyes on this particular building. Its eerie resemblance to the structure from Sara's imprisonment in my dream last night immediately caught my attention. Constructed of sturdy bricks and boasting oversized front windows, it stood in stark contrast to its neighboring buildings. Despite the slight chill that ran down my spine, what truly captivated me was the inexplicable energy emanating from within its walls. It was as if the building was beckoning me towards it. Could it be that I was subconsciously drawn to this mysterious structure, rather than simply wandering aimlessly through the city streets?

As I ascended the front stairs, my attention was captivated by the imposing front door. Unbeknownst to me, a treacherous layer of ice covered the top steps, causing me to slip as I reached the third step. Just as I was about to brace myself for impact, a pair of hands swiftly grabbed my sides from behind, causing my earbuds to fall out.

"You really should be more careful," a familiar voice said calmly.

I turned my head quickly to see who it was. "Easton?" I began in surprise. "Oh my gosh, how are you? What are you doing back? Last I heard, you moved away - without telling me, I might add!" I teased with fake annoyance.

Easton smiled. The same mischievous smile that I had grown accustomed to. "I'm sorry about that. It was a last-minute plan. If I had waited any longer, then I would have never left this place."

Smiling, I hugged him. "I forgive you," I replied jokingly. "You must tell me all about where you went and what you've been up to."

Easton's eyes dropped for a moment.

Is he upset about something?

I have known Easton since our freshman year of high school. He arrived in town as the new kid and immediately caught everyone's attention. Surprisingly, many people found him intimidating, a sentiment that I never quite understood. The guys were particularly threatened by his physical strength and envious of his good looks. With his muscular build, high cheekbones, blonde hair, and piercing green eyes, Easton became the object of desire for many girls. His gaze had a way of making you feel guilty for no apparent reason, almost as if he could see right through you. While the rest of the school felt uneasy around him, I found myself drawn to his mysterious aura.

Easton was a mysterious enigma, unlike anyone I had ever encountered. His thoughts were a locked door, impenetrable to my abilities. Initially, this unnerved me, as I was accustomed to effortlessly hearing the innermost musings of those around me. He shadowed my every move, observing me with an intensity that was both disconcerting and intriguing. Perhaps he, too, sensed something unusual about our connection.

Despite my best efforts, I could not glean a single thought from his mind. This lack of access frustrated me, but after a few weeks of contemplation, I made the bold decision to befriend him. If I couldn't unravel the mystery of his fixation on me through telepathy, I would do so through traditional means.

Ultimately, I never uncovered the rationale behind his peculiar, almost stalker-like behavior. However, in forging a friendship with Easton, I discovered a kindred spirit and gained a confidant whose thoughts remained shielded from my prying mind.

However, I never grew close enough to Easton to share my nightmares or telepathy with him. That was a secret only one person knew.

"It's really not important, Ember," he stated. "But what have you been up to since we last saw each other?"

Easton was not particularly talkative. He never spoke about himself, or much of anything for that matter.

While it would have been nice to learn more about what he had been doing over the past three years, I decided to respond to his question sarcastically. "Nothing much. You know, just living the dream. I've been job hunting and quitting multiple jobs."

He smiled and remarked, "You really aren't a people person." Easton looked past me and asked, "Do you work here?"

I turned to look at the building behind me once more. That same strange feeling radiated from within. "No, I just thought this place seemed different from all the other buildings, so I was just going to look inside," I explained.

"How does it seem different? This place has always been here. It looks a bit rougher since it has been abandoned for years, but there really isn't anything special about it," Easton replied.

"I don't know how to explain it," I stated, biting my lip.

Easton then grabbed my hand and said, "Come on, I'll show you there is nothing special about it."

We approached the building, and a strange sensation gripped my chest, causing my heart to race. Despite not feeling scared or anxious, my heart seemed to be pounding out of control.

As Easton glanced through the window, I joined him, peering into the dark and dusty interior. The room was devoid of life, filled only with overturned furniture that hinted at a past ransacking.

Just as I was considering leaving, a fleeting shadow caught my eye, sending a shiver down my spine. A wave of unease washed over me as my mind drifted back to Lucien.

"What was that?" I murmured to myself.

"What?" Easton questioned.

I shook my head. "N-nothing," I replied, fear gripping me. "Let's get out of here." The curiosity that once intrigued me has now dissipated. The thought of Lucien potentially being inside was unsettling, prompting me to leave without further investigation.

"No, now I'm curious," Easton replied with a smirk. "We should find a way inside."

"You can stay and look if you want to, but I'm leaving," I stated bluntly as I turned to walk away.

Easton grabbed my arm. "Don't leave me here. This was your idea."

"Well…" I started, "I changed my mind." I couldn't tell him why I suddenly had the urge to flee. I knew he would only laugh at me or call me crazy.

"Come on, let's find a way inside." He replied, pulling me by the arm behind him.

"Easton, I don't feel comfortable doing this," I protested. My phone started to ring as I finished my sentence. Looking at the screen, I announced, "Sorry, I have to take this."

"Where are you?" My mother's voice filled with concern asked when I answered the phone.

"I'm spending time with a friend. What's the matter?" I asked.

"Nothing," she replied quickly. "I noticed you weren't in your room... Did you have another nightmare?"

I hesitated before responding. "No," I fibbed. "I just felt like going for a walk."

My mother let out a resigned sigh. She could tell I was not being truthful. "Okay."

After reassuring my mother that everything was fine and ending the call, I turned around to locate Easton. To my surprise, he was nowhere to be seen. I searched the entire vicinity, but he was nowhere in sight. The idea that he may have found a way inside sent a shiver down my spine.

Despite my growing unease, I couldn't bring myself to enter the building. I called out Easton's name a few times while waiting for a response. As minutes passed without any sign of him, my only thought was that Easton had ditched me, so I decided to leave.

As I walked towards the front of the building, I descended the steps and entered a bustling city filled with people. The atmosphere was electric, like stepping into a crowded stadium. Time seemed to slip away unnoticed since Easton and I had climbed those steps.

My eyes darted around, trying to make sense of the cacophony of thoughts and voices blending together. The growing crowd began to take notice of me, their judgmental stares piercing through me. I felt a sense of panic and isolation, standing alone on the sidewalk. Each breath became more labored, my heart pounding erratically against my chest.

A sharp, stabbing pain shot through my chest as my heart raced out of control. Tears welled up in my eyes, my hands trembling with cold sweat. I felt trapped, unable to move as the world spun around me.

I needed to get away from everyone before I passed out, but my feet felt as if they were cemented to the sidewalk.

"Are you alright, Ember?" Easton's concerned voice broke through.

But I couldn't respond even though the voices that consumed me had stopped. *When did that happen? How long had I been standing here?* I miraculously started to calm down. My hands stopped shaking, and my breathing slowly became normal, but I still couldn't take a deep, fulfilling breath.

"Ember?" Easton called out to me, his hands gently resting on my shoulders as he stood before me. Locking eyes with me for a brief moment, he urged, "We need to leave this place." With a reassuring arm around my waist, he guided me away from the crowd, leading us down the street.

As we walked, the chaos around us began to fade, and I started to regain my composure. Finally finding my voice, I started, "Where did you disappear to?"

"I went inside the building you were curious about," Easton replied calmly.

"But I waited for you for so long," I expressed my frustration.

At first, he remained silent, gazing straight ahead and avoiding eye contact. "I just went inside to look around. When I came out, I saw you having a panic attack or something, so I hurried to help you."

I let out a sigh. "This isn't the first time I've embarrassed myself in public." It seems to happen whenever I'm caught off guard, not fully aware of my surroundings. "But I figured you ditched me while I was on the phone."

A look of confusion crossed Easton's face. "Why would I do that?"

I remained silent, hesitant to respond. Frankly, Easton appeared unreliable. Despite our friendship in high school, we never socialized outside of school, despite my efforts. Sara and I attempted to make plans with him on numerous occasions, but he never followed through. Our acquaintance was superficial at best. Unlike others, I couldn't discern his thoughts, leaving me more ignorant about him than a passing stranger. Adding to his questionable character, he disappeared without a trace shortly after graduation.

As we walked in silence, Easton suddenly interjected, "Oh, I almost forgot," rummaging through his pockets. "I found this in a room while I was exploring."

"Well, if this item was stolen, maybe we should return it. I do not want to have a stolen item," I suggested.

"It's not as if you were the one who stole it. It was found," he replied nonchalantly.

"And what if I run into the person it belongs to? It looks custom-designed." I observed, marveling at the unique gem embedded in the locket. I had never seen anything quite like it before, and while I am no expert in gemology, its otherworldly beauty was undeniable. With a sense of reverence, I handed it back to Easton.

As we strolled around, stopping at a quaint coffee shop, I couldn't help but notice a hint of irritation in his demeanor. Easton and I purchased some steaming cups of coffee and settled inside to escape the biting cold. The atmosphere between us had shifted after our little escapade, becoming tinged with an uncomfortable tension. Our exchange was stilted and terse, with Easton offering no response to my questions or attempts to spark conversation.

Raising my cup to my lips, I found myself gazing into Easton's striking emerald eyes for a prolonged moment. A nagging suspicion crept into my mind - he was hiding something. His gaze flitted away from mine after only a few seconds, unable to maintain eye contact. Sensing my scrutiny, his eyes began to dart nervously around the room.

"What's the matter?" I finally asked. "You've barely spoken since I returned the necklace."

He remained silent, steadfastly avoiding eye contact.

"What has happened to you in the past three years?" I asked, my voice tinged with worry. He had always been reserved, but he never shied away from questions and would engage in conversation during our high school days.

Easton shrugged his shoulders. "People change…" He replied dryly, "Maybe this is who I am now."

I stare at him skeptically. "Why do you avoid answering me? People don't just disappear without an explanation. They would at least lie about what they had been up to."

"Maybe I don't want to lie to you. Maybe it's just better if I don't give any explanation."

"Wow… You are just digging yourself deeper into a hole." I stared at him curiously. "Tell me, did you join a cult? A gang?" I questioned teasingly.

An amused smile played across his face.

"See, that right there!" I giggled. "You're only proving my point." I continued, slightly joking.

Easton grabbed his recent find out of his jacket pocket. "Ember, I want you to take this. I have no use for it and you are the only person who has tried to be my friend. You don't have to wear it... but just remember me when you look at it."

I was taken aback. "Whoa... Is this some kind of red flag? Do I need to call someone to have you put on a 72-hour watch?"

He chuckled. "No, I'm not that type. Now, I'm being serious Ember. Take it..."

I sighed loudly. Aggravation and defeat wash over me as I reluctantly take the locket from him. "Alright, Easton. If it's that important to you, then I'll take it."

He gave me a half-hearted smile.

"But if this bites me in the ass, then I'm coming after you."

"Understood." He replied smiling.

After Easton and I finished our coffee, we decided to go our separate ways. He was being secretive about his plans, refusing to share any details with me or anyone else. Despite my suspicions about him, I always enjoyed his company because it allowed me to escape from reality, if only for a little while.

Once I returned home, I took the new necklace out of my pocket and examined it closely. The locket was truly remarkable, with a blue jewel that seemed to emit an orange light as I gazed into it. The light grew brighter and more intense the longer I focused on it, and I couldn't help but feel a sense of unease. There was also something else… A noise?

The sound emanating from the jewel resembled a scratching noise, as though someone was dragging their fingernails along its interior. The longer I gazed at the object, the more pronounced the noise grew, captivating me with its enigmatic allure. I found myself unable to look away.

Abruptly, a sharp rap at my door shattered my concentration, causing me to startle and drop the locket. The sudden and jarring sound snapped me back to reality.

"Ember, Sara is here to see you!" My mother's voice called from the other side of the door.

Chapter Three

Secrets

"Coming!" I yelled back, hastily picking up the locket. With a glance, I realized it was just an ordinary gem - no orange light or scratching noise. *Was I imagining things?* I wondered as I placed it back on my dresser. Just then, Sara burst in, clearly agitated.

"Where have you been?" she demanded, arms crossed.

"Well, hello, Sara. How are you today? Isn't the weather lovely?" I replied sarcastically. "I only got home about an hour ago. What's going on?"

"You were supposed to meet me for lunch, remember?" She replied angrily. "I tried calling you a thousand times!"

I glanced at my phone in disbelief. "It never rang..." I couldn't believe I had forgotten about our lunch plans. "I'm truly sorry, Sara," I began to apologize. "I woke up early and decided to go for a walk. I must have completely forgotten when I ran into Easton..."

"Easton?" Sara muttered, her expression turning ashen as she collapsed onto my bed as if struck by a sudden blow. The color drained from her face as her thoughts raced erratically, overwhelming us both.

I sat beside her and said, "Sara, you need to calm down. What's the matter?"

She didn't respond to my question right away. It wasn't until some of the color returned to her face that she started, "What is he doing back?"

"I don't know..." I responded questioningly. *Why did she care that much about Easton's return?* "He wouldn't tell me anything. Hell, he hardly even spoke to me, to be honest. There seems to be something wrong with him or... I don't know... He was acting stranger than usual."

Sadness filled Sara's eyes as she asked, "Where did you meet him?"

"Why are you so concerned about him?" I demanded, rising to my feet. "You stormed in here furious because I unintentionally stood you up, and the moment Easton's name is brought up, you fall apart. What's happening?"

Sara shook her head, forcing a smile as she replied, "It's not a big deal. Did you have one of your nightmares?"

"Oh no, you're not going to change the subject that easily," I stated firmly.

She got up from the bed and walked over to the window. "I just don't want to talk about it right now, Ember…"

"Alright, but you ARE going to tell me about it… One way or another…" I threatened.

Sara spun around on her heel. "You promised that you would NEVER do that!"

"Hey, if someone you barely knew had this much effect on your best friend, I think you would do the same." I retorted in defense.

"Some things are meant to be private, Ember!" You cannot just pick stuff from people's heads on a whim! It's not fair that you can know everything about everyone while you are allowed to keep your own secrets."

Sara and I have been best friends since our days in Kindergarten. I remember meeting her when she was going through a tough time at home and struggling to make new friends. She was a sweet young girl with a flushed face and long blonde hair styled in braided pig-tails. Now, as I look at her, I see a grown woman with a face red with anger - anger directed towards me because of our differences. I made the foolish mistake of threatening to reveal a secret about her and Easton, one she held close to her heart.

Sara was the only person who knew about my unique abilities. Unfortunately, this knowledge led to distrust from her, as sometimes her thoughts unintentionally slipped out. It's not a common occurrence, but it does happen. Some thoughts are so intrusive and brazen that they cannot be contained.

I'm not sure if it is because of how close we are that I managed to keep her thoughts at bay. Lately, I only hear her thoughts when she is upset or when we are physically close.

Strangely, physical touch seems to amplify not only her thoughts but others as well.

Over the years, my parents' inner voices have quieted down, but not as much as Sara's. But there were always times when my parents or my friend would become emotional and I could hear them loud and clear…

Feeling speechless and guilty after my outburst, Sara walked over to my dresser and noticed the locket I had placed there before she arrived. She picked it up and examined it closely.

"This is a very beautiful necklace… Where did you get it?"

Before answering, I contemplated my answer. Should I be honest or just lie? After the way she reacted to Easton being back in town, I wasn't sure if I should say. But, then again, I have always detested dishonesty. "Easton found it in an unusual place today." I hesitantly replied. "He said he had no use for it and told me to keep it."

Her eyes lingered on the jewel before placing it back down. Clearing her throat, she continued, "It's very beautiful." She sat down on the bed with me following right behind her. "So, are you two a couple now?" Her voice cracked.

"What?" I asked incredulously. "No! Today was the first time I had seen him in years. You know I have a weird feeling about him..." Then a thought dawned on me. "Wait... Do you have a thing for him?"

Sara's face turned as red as a tomato.

"Really?" I asked in astonishment. "You two would've made a cute couple in high school."

Tears started to stream down her face.

"What's wrong?"

"I thought you knew..." She sobbed. "I just assumed you knew and kept it to yourself like you always do..."

"What?" I replied confused. *Was there something I was supposed to know?*

"Easton and I were together in high school…"

I stood up and stared at her in doubt. The confusion I felt changed to a feeling of betrayal. "How? When? What happened? And why the hell didn't you tell me?" *Why wouldn't she tell me something like that? That seems silly to hide.*

"I thought you knew… You know everything…" she repeated.

"Apparently, I don't. I told you I couldn't hear everything you were thinking. And I also told you I couldn't hear anything from Easton from the beginning. I was honest with you when I said your thoughts mostly bleed through if I touch you."

Sara let out a drawn-out sigh and grabbed my hand. "Concentrate. Then you will know everything…" She let out another sob. "It's easier than talking…"

"Are you sure?" I questioned hesitantly, not wanting to get lost in other thoughts she was having.

She nodded. "You deserve to know…"

"Fine…" I replied in defeat. "You focus on what's making you feel this way so I don't wander into other thoughts…"

I am not an expert at this at all. I've unintentionally done this one other time and I was not entirely sure how I had done it. It would be nice if there was some kind of manual on how this stuff works.

For the first few minutes, nothing happened. I was just staring at the back of my eyelids. I was about to give up when Easton's face flashed before me. I was reliving Sara's memories. I could feel all of the emotions that she felt and hear everything that was going on around her. It was like I traveled back to freshman year in high school, except I was Sara. We wore our school uniforms – white button-up blouses and hunter-green pleated skirts.

I turn to look at my past self through Sara's eyes. *This is so weird…*

We talked about some nonsense that had just happened with some of our classmates. Then the room grew quiet when Easton appeared at the entrance. Sara's heart started to race as his intense green eyes stared through me. His blonde hair was styled with a spikiness to it. *She was checking him out!*

As Sara, I found it hard to catch my breath and anxiety began to consume me. Sara's eyes glanced over to high school me. Her voice rang in my ears, *"Ember must like him too… She is studying him as much as I am."*

Just as quickly as I saw this memory, it passed. I was then teleported to a time when Sara sat alone in the cafeteria until my past self walked up to sit with her.

I looked at my old self, as Sara, and began, "Do you find the new guy interesting?"

High school Ember replied, "I find that there is… something interesting about him," pausing to take a bite of lunch. "Why do you ask?"

"No reason, really... I have just noticed that you have been spending a lot of time with him these past few weeks..."

"Well, it's not exactly by choice, Sara. You know that. I don't even see him after school or know anything about him. He just happens to be in all my classes."

"Why do you say that he is interesting then?"

Before high school Ember answered, she looked around to make sure no one was listening or near us before leaning closer to Sara and continuing quietly, "I just don't trust him. He freaks me out. I've never experienced this situation before."

Sara's eyes wandered away from her face and rested on Easton, who was staring at her from the back of the cafeteria. I could feel my face becoming warm.

Past me continued, almost as a dull murmur in the background. "I can't hear his or anyone's thoughts when he is around..."

Sara's heart must have weighed heavy at this remark because I was suddenly consumed by sadness. "Well… sounds like you two would make a great couple…" She began, looking back at me with a feeling of disappointment. "Maybe there's a chance you won't have to put up with your abilities 24/7 now."

"What, and use him? That wouldn't make me any better than the rest of these people." I remarked, rolling my eyes and taking a sip of my soda. "I mean, he is attractive, but I'm not interested in him like that. My interest in him is more figuring out a science experiment than anything else."

She giggled at this. "Are you calling him a freak of nature?" Her eyes moved back to her eye candy. He was smiling as if he was chuckling to himself about something. But what? He wasn't sitting with anyone.

I laughed at her question. "No, not exactly. That wouldn't be fair to call him that. I mean, look at me."

Another few months flew past, and a barrage of faces, voices, colors, and shapes whizzed past, making me feel a little disoriented until it slowed, and I found myself as Sara sitting alone in the lunchroom once again during junior year.

I noticed someone walking towards me and looked up to find Easton smiling back at me. "Hello," he stated.

A smile spread across my face. I could feel Sara's giddiness mixed with anxiety. "Hi."

"So, where's your friend, Ember?" he asked.

"She isn't feeling well today."

"Oh," Easton replied with a little disappointment in his voice. "May I sit with you?" He asked politely.

"Yes!" She said overly excited. Her face grew hot as she let her true awkward feelings show.

He only smiled at her as he took his seat. "So, how long have you and Ember been friends?"

"Since we were about... six years old, maybe. We met in Kindergarten."

"That must be nice to have a friend for a decade... I've never had that."

"Why not?"

He shrugged. "My family moves around a lot."

"I'm sorry to hear that... Ember and I have just stuck together for so long because we don't fit in anywhere else. Well, I mean, we are best friends because we have a lot in common, but we also don't really fit in anywhere else either."

He smiled at her. "I couldn't help but come over to you. I know we have been coming to the same school for two years now, but... I always noticed you... Even the very first day I walked in. I immediately saw you."

I could feel Sara's face become hot again. Staring deeply into his eyes, she didn't say a word. Nor did any thoughts cross her mind.

Before I could fully grasp what was happening between them, I was thrown through another multitude of memories. Various dates Sara and Easton had been on flashed before my eyes: kissing and… intimate moments I wish I could unsee passed by.

Finally, it was graduation night. Sara and I were still in our gowns, playfully bantering as we were ready to leave. Suddenly, Easton emerged from behind a nearby tree, catching Sara's attention. She quickly excused herself, mentioning that she needed to speak with her mother. I left as she made her way over to Easton.

She embraced him, but he did not move an inch.

His complexion was pale, and a look of anguish was etched on his face.

"What's wrong?" Sara asked, her heart racing at the sight of his sorrowful expression. This was a side of him she had never witnessed before.

"Let's find a quiet place," he replied hesitantly. "There's something important I need to tell you." Easton's voice carried a sense of urgency, yet there was a hint of harshness in his tone. It was clear that whatever he needed to discuss, wasn't something he was looking forward to.

Sara's heart sank at his words, tears welling up in her eyes. She already had a sinking feeling about what was coming. Despite her reluctance, she followed him away from the crowd of recently graduated seniors and into the empty parking lot, where they sat in his car.

Silent and immobile, Sara sat in the vehicle, feeling as though she had lost all ability to function.

Easton cleared his throat. "I'm having to leave for a while," he stated slowly, "and with where I need to go, it's best that we..." He trailed off, struggling to find the right words. After a moment of silence, he took a deep breath and continued, "I feel that it's best that we break up."

As soon as the words left his lips, tears welled up in Sara's eyes, cascading down her cheeks. She couldn't bring herself to meet his gaze. "Where are you going?" she asked, her voice flat and resigned. She knew that no amount of pleading would change his mind. Sara was not one to beg, no matter how much she desired a different outcome.

"I can't tell you that," he stated bluntly. "Please, Sara, trust me when I say that this is the last thing I want to do," Easton pleaded, longing to comfort her, but understanding that he couldn't.

"Why are you doing this, then?" Her voice trembled as she questioned him.

Easton gazed at her, but she avoided his eyes. "I can't explain... It's for your safety."

"Then it's over," she replied icily as she opened the car door.

Before she could leave, Easton reached out and grabbed her hand. "Sara... I love you," he confessed, tears welling up in his eyes.

She jerked her arm away from him and walked off by herself.

In an instant, I found myself back in my room. Tears welled up in my eyes, blurring my vision. Releasing Ruth's hand, I gazed at her in shock. "You kept a serious relationship and breakup a secret from me for five years?" Anger seeped into my voice. "I am your best friend! Do you seriously not trust me that much?"

"It wasn't like that!"

"What possible reason could you have for not divulging something like that? Did you think I wouldn't approve?"

She gazed down at her feet, a mixture of guilt and shame etched on her face. "I... I don't have a good explanation..."

"You must have some sort of reasoning. Especially since you couldn't tell me you two broke up on graduation day! You told me you were sick!"

Sara sighed heavily, brushing away the tears that threatened to spill over. "Easton wanted me to keep it a secret... I didn't understand why. At first, I thought he was ashamed of me, but he convinced me that wasn't the case. He just didn't want you to know. I asked for a specific reason. Maybe he had feelings for you or he didn't like you. But he denied all that, claiming he thought you wouldn't like him dating your best friend or some other excuse... I assumed you already knew, even before he asked I keep it a secret..." She rose from the bed and began fiddling with the locket on the dresser again.

Her explanation left me dumbfounded. It didn't seem like a good reason to keep something this big from me.

"You know... you two aren't all that different," she suddenly stated.

"What do you mean by that?" I asked more offensively than I intended it to come out.

"Easton is telepathic also."

I was taken aback by her confession. "I had no idea..." Suddenly, fear gripped me. "You didn't tell him I was, did you?"

Sara offered a weak smile. "That's not my secret to share. I tried my best not to think about you when he was around. I also tried my best not to make any connections between the two of you while I was around him. He never brought you up, so I believe you're in the clear."

I didn't say anything more as I watched her play with that locket. Today had been very exhausting for me. How could so much happen in one day? More importantly, how could I not have known any of this was happening? Am I losing my touch? That should be something that I am excited about, but it made me more concerned.

Why would Easton want to keep all of it a secret? What was he playing at? There was something about all of this that was wrong and deeply unsettling. Maybe I was right to be suspicious of him all along.

"You can have the locket if you want," I finally broke the silence, getting up from the bed and walking over to Sara.

"No, it's yours," she replied with a sigh.

"To be honest, after seeing him through your eyes and knowing how you felt about him, I'd rather not have it." It was a haunting feeling to have loved and lost in a matter of seconds. Even though it wasn't actually me, I still experienced it all.

I had never had a boyfriend, but now I know the emptiness that came from the sting of your first love.

"Well, I don't want it." She retorted, still looking at the jewelry. "Especially not to be reminded of *him*."

"Fair enough," I replied. "But now I don't want it to be reminded of him. Now all I will see is a naked Easton.." I gagged.

Sara's face blushed with embarrassment. "You saw that? Oh no…"

"It's fine," I replied. "Kind of, I guess. My poor eyes…"

Sara covered her face with her hands as I continued teasing her.

"I'm kidding Sara, chill." I giggled, trying to lighten the mood.

We remained quiet for a minute, before a thought occurred to me, "Sara, has this jewel looked strange to you in the whole time you have been holding it?"

"The only thing that strikes me as odd is that I have never seen anything like it." She replied.

"No… It's not that," I stated, grabbing it from her hand.

"Then what?" She asked curiously, inspecting it with me.

I stared at it for a minute. "Nothing," I replied, looking at it harder. This time, it didn't do anything. "It must have been my imagination."

Chapter Four

It Begins

Not only was I already running on very little sleep, but life decided to throw me a curveball when Easton returned. He left me with a whirlwind of perplexing questions, particularly about a mysterious locket. My best friend had kept her relationship with Easton a secret from me for five years before suddenly revealing the truth. Needless to say, I have been on an emotional rollercoaster since I woke up that morning.

The events of that day had left me feeling drained and overwhelmed as if my nerves were completely fried. Little did I know, things were about to become even more complicated.

Sara and I stayed hidden in my room away from my parents. It's not that I didn't get along with my parents, it's just I didn't want to be wrapped up in whatever was going on with them. My parents suspected I could hear their thoughts, especially as a toddler, I didn't realize they weren't speaking aloud. However, I quickly learned not to comment on their internal musings. This unspoken understanding created a sense of distance between us, one that made me believe our relationship was strained. It wasn't necessarily negative, but rather a result of our conflicting personalities.

My mother worked as a secretary, and my father is a mechanic who owns his own shop. I have an older brother named Will, but we haven't seen or heard from him in over a year. He did not get along with my parents at all. Our mom could be quick and rash, sometimes over-emotional, while Will was calm and always kept situations from escalating. I admired my brother's ability to wear his heart on his sleeve.

The last time I spoke to Will was the night he moved out. He was upset because he didn't want to leave me behind, but he felt he had no other choice. He urged me to go with him, but I couldn't bear to leave everything familiar to me, especially Sara. It's not easy for someone like me to make friends, let alone find someone who truly understands the weight I carry.

When I expressed my reluctance to move away, he struggled to comprehend my feelings and continued to encourage me to go with him. Will was overwhelmed with guilt for leaving me behind, but the challenges he faced with my parents became too much for him to bear, which contributed to his decision to leave.

After Sara and I finished our conversation, we decided to leave my house and go exploring at our favorite shops before stopping for a bite to eat. While in town, we were at the bookstore, thumbing through novels when my phone began to ring.

As I rummaged through my purse in search of my phone, I noticed a shiny object lying next to it. Despite my phone's insistent ringing, I was drawn to the gleaming item and reached for it.

"How did this get in my purse?" I murmured to myself as I pulled the locket out.

"You stuck it in there before we left the house," Sara replied mindlessly as she grabbed a book to read its summary.

"I don't remember doing that," I mumbled.

She didn't respond to my statement, keeping her face buried in the book.

I placed the necklace back in my purse, not giving it another thought. Looking at my phone, I saw that my mother had called. It was strange she was calling so soon after we left but she could wait. Letting out a sigh, I started, "We need to leave soon..." I told Sara, "I'm starting to get a headache from this crowd."

"Ok, I'm starting to get hungry anyway."

We started dressing in our coats, gloves, and scarves before venturing outside, making our way to our favorite little restaurant. Upon entering, Sara and I brushed off our feet on the rug by the door and took in the cozy atmosphere. The restaurant was relatively empty, as it was not yet dinner time.

A small group of teenagers occupied a booth in the back, chatting animatedly by the window. Meanwhile, three individuals sat at the bar, leisurely enjoying their meals and sipping coffee while engaging in light conversation.

Sara and I made our way to a table at the center of the diner, placing our coats, scarves, and gloves on the back of our chairs. A waitress walked up, asked if we wanted our usual. We were more than happy to say yes!

While we got settled at our table, someone walked through the entrance, causing the entire atmosphere to shift. A sense of unease crept over me, yet I found myself strangely calm amidst the anxiety that gripped me.

Sara's eyes flitted nervously around the room, avoiding eye contact with someone. Her cheeks flushed with color as she repeatedly glanced behind me, growing increasingly agitated before my eyes.

"What's the matter?" I asked, preparing to turn and face whatever had caught her attention. In truth, a sense of fear grew within me.

"It's nothing. Don't worry about it." She responded, looking down at her hands.

I shrugged, relieved I wouldn't have to face whatever was making her nervous. *Hopefully, it isn't Easton,* I thought to myself. Then I realized, I couldn't hear anyone once again today. *Maybe he is here...* I grew increasingly concerned for my friend as a surge of emotions washed over me.

Strangely, I felt a sense of security, yet my heart began to race and my face flushed. Butterflies violently fluttered in my stomach, causing a mix of anxiety and nausea.

I glanced at Sara, who could clearly see the fear in my eyes as I silently mouthed, "I can't hear anything," to her. Her eyes widened and quickly shifted to the area behind me. "What's wrong?" I whispered quietly to my friend.

Her true answer caught me off guard as she whispered, "There is a very hot guy sitting behind you... He hasn't taken his eyes off you since he entered."

My face was still flushed as the waitress interrupted our awkward conversation by bringing us our food. My heart was still racing, and the whole situation was unnerving. I made a conscious effort not to look behind me, resisting the urge with every fiber of my being. Sara's frequent glances at the mysterious person only fueled my growing curiosity. The suspense was becoming unbearable.

Midway through our meal, the waitress approached the table where the "hot" guy was seated, and asked for his order. The man responded, but I couldn't hear his words because I recognized the voice. My heart sank as chills ran down my spine.

This cannot be real, I thought to myself. Sara noticed my sudden stillness and became worried.

"Ember? Are you feeling alright?"

"Y-yeah…" I replied sheepishly.

"Are you sure?" She questioned, looking at me skeptically. "You are very pale now."

"I'll tell you about it later…" I said, unable to comprehend what was going on. I figured I could at least catch a glimpse of the guy to dismiss the thought that sprang to mind.

Sara leaned over the table after a few minutes and started speaking quietly. "Don't you want to take a look at the guy?"

"Of course I do." I quietly admitted.

"You better hurry. I think he might leave soon."

Following her advice, I took a deep breath before casually dropping my knife to the floor. As I leaned over to pick it up, I stole a glance at the person nearby. His face took my breath away, with beautiful eyes that seemed to pierce through me as a smirk played on his lips. Quickly tearing my gaze away, I turned to Sara with urgency in my voice.

"We need to leave," I said earnestly, my heart racing.

"Why?" Sara asked, confusion evident in her voice as I hastily gathered my belongings.

"No, no, no, no…. This isn't happening…" I threw some money on the table and grabbed my things.

"Ember, calm down and wait for me!" Sara called after me, quickly grabbing her things.

I hurried out of the diner, deliberately avoiding the man who had unsettled me. Despite my efforts to shake off the encounter, I couldn't escape the sensation of his eyes following me.

As Sara and I stepped outside, I quickened my pace, leaving her struggling to keep up. She called out to me, demanding an explanation. "Ember, slow down! What happened back there? Ember, please wait!"

I was determined to keep moving forward without stopping to talk. Despite my efforts to hold onto my doubts, deep down, I knew that what I had just witnessed was undeniably true.

"Ember!" I heard Sara call out, her voice filled with urgency as she grabbed my arm. "Who was that?"

I came to a halt and paused to take a deep breath. "Last night, I had a dream that a man who looked strikingly similar to the one we just saw... The resemblance is uncanny..." A sharp pain began to throb in my head as I tried to make sense of it all. "I usually have the same recurring nightmare with the shadow man chasing me, but last night, that man from the diner was there. He saved me from him..."

Sara's eyes looked like they were about to pop out of her head. "That... That is very strange..."

My heart kept racing as I remembered the dream; his eyes.

"Normally, I would say that maybe it was only a coincidence..." Sara began, "But I don't think coincidences happen with you very often..." She noticed the look on my face and added, "No offense."

"I figured as much..." I replied with a groan.

"Well, maybe... Maybe we should go back and ask him about it?" Sara suggested eagerly, her voice filled with enthusiasm.

The thought of this terrified me. If he was real... then that would mean the shadow man was real also.

"If I was to do as you said, what would I even say? 'I'm sorry to bother you, but I had a dream about you last night, and you saved me from an evil shadow man named Lucien.' Do you know how crazy that sounds?"

Sara giggled. "You're right, but I think it would still be worth a shot. Either way, it is a very creative pick-up line."

I rolled my eyes at my friend. "To be honest, at first I thought you might've seen Easton."

"See, I think we should go ask him about this stuff. There definitely has to be something going on."

There was something undeniably wrong with this entire situation. I looked into the faces of the passersby and realized I still could not hear what they were thinking. He had to be following us. But I didn't feel like we were in danger. "Well, we won't have to go back to the diner to ask," I remarked.

Sara looked at me questioningly.

"He's been following us since we left the diner."

Sara spun around on her heel to see. "How do you know? I can't see anyone."

"Because I still don't have my telepathy."

"What do we do?" She asked nervously. Losing all her nerves from earlier.

"We go to the park and wait for him to show," I stated with dread. "He obviously wants to talk or have some type of interaction… He'll eventually come up to me.

As we walked towards the park, a heavy silence hung between us. The clock had struck six, and the biting winter air seemed to pierce through our jackets as we settled onto a bench. Our bodies shivered involuntarily, our breath forming clouds in the freezing weather. The snow fell steadily, adding to the thick blanket already covering the ground.

Despite the cold, we sat in silence, our eyes scanning the park for any sign of Aiden. People who noticed us, stared as if we were lunatics for sitting out in the freezing weather. But after less than half an hour of waiting, the cold became unbearable, and we could no longer ignore it.

"Ember, I don't know how much longer I can wait. I can not feel my nose, fingers, or my toes!" Sara stated through chattering teeth.

"Ok," I stated while staying on the bench. "Why don't you go get us some coffee or hot chocolate across the street and warm up?"

"What about you?" she asked.

"I won't be too far behind you," I replied. I had a sneaking suspicion that Aiden wouldn't approach me with Sara near me.

I could see that Sara was torn between waiting for me and leaving.

"Sara, go! It's fine." I giggled.

She didn't wait for any more explanations as to why I wasn't going with her as she scurried across the street.

I sat waiting for my hero to show his face. Ten minutes passed by and the snow grew denser when I finally decided he wasn't going to approach me, or rather, I wasn't going to wait in the weather any longer.

"You're going to catch pneumonia sitting out in this weather, my love."

I was taken aback, my stomach dropping and a wave of nausea washing over me for a brief moment as my eyes widened in surprise. I turned my head sharply in the direction of the voice that had startled me. It was Aiden. I studied him intently - his shaggy black hair mostly hidden under a beanie, his greenish-yellow eyes just like in my dream, and a smile on his face that revealed perfectly white teeth.

"You're the one who took your time to come talk to me," I finally stated once I caught my breath.

Aiden smirked at my quip.

"How–"

"Am I here?" He finished my question. "I've always existed, Ember. The reason you had not seen me before last night is because I had finally found you."

"How did you find me? What do you want? Why doesn't my telepathy work when you're around? Why are you here? Is that shadow man, Lucien, real?" All of these burning questions flooded out of my mouth.

"Whoa, calm down, love," Aiden responded, drawing closer to me. "We have plenty of time to talk about everything." He placed his hand on my cheek, stroking it with his thumb. This gesture, coupled with his affectionate gaze, and smile made me feel comforted.

Normally, I hate it when people touch me, but there was something about his touch that made me feel at ease. As Aiden gazed into my eyes, my heart raced and my stomach fluttered. There was a longing in his eyes, a desire that I couldn't quite comprehend at that moment. It felt familiar, reminiscent of the connection I had sensed between Sara and Easton earlier that day.

Silently, we stood locked in a gaze, the world around us fading into the background. Time seemed to freeze, leaving us suspended in a moment of shared intensity. When we finally snapped back to reality, we must have appeared like two statues, frozen in time amidst a flurry of snow.

His gaze abruptly shifted towards the coffee shop where Sara was, and he leaned in close to whisper in my ear, "I'll meet you at your place tonight. Just you, okay?"

"How do you know where I live?" I asked, but he only smiled in return.

Before leaving, he planted a kiss on my cheek. My face flushed with warmth as I watched him disappear into the darkness of the night.

"Did he ever show up?" Sara walked up without me noticing, making me jump.

"Yeah…"

"What did he say?" She questioned excitedly.

"Nothing really…"

Her expression twisted in disappointment, "Seriously?"

After taking a moment to reflect, I announced, "I think I'm going to head home."

Sara's response was filled with concern. "Are you sure? Do you want me to come with you?"

"No, I think I just need to get some rest," I explained. "Today has been incredibly draining. I can barely even think straight anymore."

"Alright," Sara said, offering me a comforting hug. "I'll see you tomorrow after work then."

I knew I could have confided in Sara about the true reason I wanted to be alone, and I was confident she would have been understanding. However, at that moment, I simply wasn't ready to delve into the details

with her. I did not know enough about what
was happening to explain everything.

Chapter Five

Aiden

When I arrived home, I was greeted by the comforting warmth emanating from the crackling fire in the fireplace. The sensation was a welcome relief to my freezing skin, which had begun to cause my joints to ache. The heat enveloped me, causing my eyes to grow heavy and a yawn to escape my lips. Standing before the fireplace, I basked in the cozy atmosphere, only to notice the eerie silence that permeated the house. It was unusual for this hour.

My parents typically stay up late, so I assumed they were home when I noticed the warm glow of a fire emanating from the fireplace. *Strange… Maybe they decided to go to bed early?*

After putting the fire out, I start toward my room. This is when I noticed a note on the coffee table.

'We had an urgent call that we needed to go take care of. Not sure when we will be back. Don't wait up and have pleasant dreams.

Love, Mom and Dad'

Well, that's unusual... I thought as I set the note back down. Realizing I was alone at home, I checked the doors to ensure they were locked before heading to my bedroom to unwind.

After changing into my pajamas, I felt the fatigue from the day setting in. I turned on the TV, struggling to keep my eyes open. Just as I was on the verge of falling asleep, a knocking sound at my window startled me. I turned to look and nearly jumped out of my skin when I saw Aiden's face peering back at me.

Geez… I'm up now…

I opened the window and helped him climb inside before asking, "How long have you been out there?" I quickly shut out the cold. Allowing a stranger into my room late at night may not have been the wisest decision, but there was something oddly *familiar* about him.

"Not long at all," he replied with a charming smile, removing his snow-covered coat and beanie.

My face flushed with embarrassment as I asked, "Did– Did you see me undress?"

He responded with a sly smile, increasing my mortification.

Aiden gently took my hands and guided me to the bed, where we sat beside each other. Surprisingly, the atmosphere was far from awkward; I felt an unusual sense of comfort and security in his presence. Each time his hand made contact with mine, a jolt of electricity seemed to course through my body, sending shivers down my spine. But there was something more, a strange sensation in the pit of my stomach that compelled me to draw closer to him.

As I made this realization, I gazed into his mesmerizing eyes. My heart began to race, nerves tingling. Swallowing hard, I finally spoke up, "How did you know where I live?" I asked, attempting to break the silence that had settled between us.

"I didn't," he smiled, adding, "I followed you."

"That's not creepy…" I replied sarcastically.

"I know it sounds creepy, but I promise I'm not a creep." He responded with the most beautiful laugh I ever heard.

"How did you know where I was? You couldn't have been following me all day," I questioned.

"You don't realize how long I've been searching for you, Ember," he replied.

I gazed at him, puzzled, waiting for him to explain further.

He reclined on the bed, gazing at the ceiling before gently taking my arm and saying, "Lay down with me, my love."

An instinctual feeling assured me that it was safe to lie down beside him. Perhaps he would finally provide answers to my questions without resorting to cryptic riddles. As I nestled next to him, his arm enveloped me, drawing me closer until my head rested on his chest. My heart quickened its pace as I listened to his steady heartbeat. The sensation of being in such close proximity to someone, feeling their touch, stirred a mix of nerves and excitement within me, emotions I never thought I would experience.

Despite my reluctance for the moment to end, there remained a multitude of unanswered questions lingering in my mind. Raising myself up, I gazed at him, yearning to lock eyes with him, but he kept them shut, seemingly relishing the moment.

I scrutinized his serene countenance. Aiden possessed prominent cheekbones and a nose of moderate size that harmonized with his facial features. A faint scar traced a path from just above his right eyebrow, crossing through it and leaving a small bald spot in its wake. After a period of silently observing his visage, I mustered the courage to speak, "How is it that you manage to silence everything and everyone when you are near me?"

Without opening his eyes, he responded nonchalantly, "I create a protective barrier around myself that extends to encompass you as well. This barrier aids in focusing on specific individuals you wish to hear."

"Wait... You're telepathic as well?" I asked, surprised.

"Of course, my love," he replied.

I couldn't help but smile when he referred to me as his love. "Why do you call me that?"

"What do you mean?" he asked.

"Why do you call me 'love'?" I clarified.

Aiden opened his eyes and gazed at me. "Because you are," he said, a hint of sadness in his eyes. "Does it bother you?"

"It probably should," I began, "but strangely, it doesn't."

He let out a sigh as if he had been holding his breath.

Aiden's smile was warm as he gently brushed his thumb against my cheek.

"How can you be sure that I am the one you love? What if I have a boyfriend I'm madly in love with?"

His smile widened with a playful glint in his eyes. "Are you suggesting I have competition?"

"Maybe you do." I teased.

Aiden's eyes sparkled as he spoke, his words filled with confidence. "I know that you are not currently in a relationship. Your thoughts are like an open book, a quality we may need to address." He paused, carefully choosing his words. "It can be challenging for individuals like us to connect with 'normal' people... And I may have taken a peek into your mind, just a little bit." He chuckled softly.

"Wow... now I understand how Sara must feel."

With a smile still on his face, he continued, "I didn't do that to uncover anything too personal. However, you must focus on developing a mental lock for your thoughts. Anyone with our abilities could easily extract information from you."

"And you intend to teach me how to create this mental barrier?" I asked in disbelief.

"Yes."

Feeling a sense of relief, I couldn't help but be grateful that Aiden could guide me in learning how to control my abilities.

"The barrier is something I will need to teach you about soon. As for everything else, I cannot go into all the details right now," he continued, gently brushing some hair behind my ear with his fingers.

As he spoke, I felt a wave of drowsiness wash over me, but I fought to stay awake in his presence. The silence between us did not help the sleepiness I felt.

"When I was six years old, I began having dreams. These dreams showed me a beautiful girl with brunette hair and the most striking blue eyes I had ever seen. After experiencing these dreams repeatedly, I realized that they were not mere figments of my imagination. They were memories."

Confusion filled me as I looked up at him, the sleepiness fading away. "Memories?"

He shook his head. "You haven't had any?"

"No… Only nightmares with my shadow man."

Aiden's expression twisted when I referred to Lucien as 'my shadow man.' "It's different every time…" he murmured, more to himself than to me. But I couldn't resist interrupting his train of thought.

"What do you mean it's different every time? What are you trying to say?" I felt my frustration growing. Aiden's words were becoming increasingly mysterious. Every question I asked only seemed to lead to more questions.

He gazed back at me with patience and warmth. "Don't worry about it now, my love," Aiden reassured me, pulling me closer. "Let's just savor the time we have together in this moment."

I found myself unable to resist Aiden's suggestion as he gently guided my chin towards his, drawing me in for a kiss. Despite any doubts I may have had, I was certain that this moment was meant to be; it just felt so right.

Aiden now lay atop me on my bed, his hands exploring every contour of my skin as our passionate embrace continued. The sensation of electricity surged through me with each touch, sending shivers down my spine. I ran my fingers through his hair, yearning to pull him closer. As our connection deepened, I felt myself losing control, breathless and overwhelmed by the intensity of his touch.

His hand lingered on my waist, then boldly moved up my shirt, tracing the curves he knew so well. A shiver ran through me as his fingers brushed my skin, and I couldn't suppress a soft moan when his lips found my neck. The world faded away, leaving only the intoxicating sensation of his touch.

All I wanted was more, to feel him closer, to lose myself in the moment. Logic faded, replaced by an inexplicable trust. He made my heart pound, my breath quicken, and I felt a connection that defied reason.

His hand descended, finding its way to the curve of my hip, eliciting another involuntary sound. As we lay there, wrapped in the heat of desire, he pulled away, his gaze intense.

"I've waited for this," he breathed, his voice husky with longing. "Searched for you for years." His eyes burned with a passion that mirrored my own. "I have to stop before I lose control."

I pouted playfully, a smile tugging at his lips.

He leaned in for a tender kiss, then rolled onto his side, our bodies intertwined. We lay there, lost in each other's eyes, the silence filled with unspoken promises.

Lost in his gaze, every question I had melted away. His eyes held a deep longing, a love so pure, that nothing else mattered.

"I'm here," I whispered, yearning for his touch. "Your search is over." I shed my shirt, inviting him to take what he desired.

His eyes widened, a mix of shock and desire flashing across his face. I could feel his internal struggle, the battle between restraint and passion. Yet, despite my teasing, he held back, content with holding me close through the night.

"This feeling... it's unlike anything I've ever experienced," I sighed, my voice soft. "It's as if our souls are intertwined."

Aiden's gaze held mine. "In my world, this is the mark of a true soulmate. A bond that transcends time and space."

****

I awoke later, still enveloped in Aiden's embrace. My head was nestled against his chest, his arms securely wrapped around me. As I gazed at him, a sense of peace washed over me. However, my attention was soon drawn to a peculiar glow emanating from my purse.

An orange light pulsated from where my purse lay. With a sense of curiosity, I rose from the bed and hastily put on my shirt. Retrieving my purse, I reached for the locket within. To my surprise, the unidentifiable blue gem within the locket was once again emitting an enchanting orange light.

"What on earth are you?" I whispered to myself, captivated by the necklace.

Aiden stirred in his sleep, causing me to quickly conceal the locket I held in my hand.

"What is that?" his gruff voice asked.

"It's nothing, just go back to sleep—" I began to respond, but he was already standing beside me, his gaze fixed on the locket.

"Where did you get this?" His voice took on a stern tone, demanding an explanation.

"Someone gave it to me," I replied sheepishly.

He snatched it from my hand, his fingers tracing the intricate design. "Who gave this to you?"

"Easton," I said, my voice barely a whisper.

A dark cloud settled over his face at the name. "Easton?" he repeated, his voice laced with a dangerous undertone. "I'm too late..." He turned away, his figure shrouded in shadows.

"What do you mean, 'too late'?" I asked, my voice trembling. "Where are you going? Aiden, please, what's wrong?" Tears welled up in my eyes, a mix of fear and confusion.

He whirled around, his eyes burning with intensity. "I won't be long, my love. I have something to attend to, someone to confront." He leaned in, his lips brushing mine. "Don't worry, I'll be back before you know it."

"But why are you so secretive? What's going on with Easton?" I demanded, my curiosity piqued.

He hesitated, his gaze distant. "Easton and I share a complicated history. He's not to be trusted."

"But I've known him for years!" I protested. "He's never done anything wrong."

A flicker of pain crossed his face. "You don't know the half of it," he said, his voice low. "There's more to Easton than meets the eye."

"I opened my mouth to respond, but the words caught in my throat. Aiden was right. I knew nothing about Easton. He was a shadow, a mystery. Even when I was in Sara's mind, he remained a closed book. "So how do you know him?" I asked, my voice barely a whisper.

He didn't answer, his gaze fixed on something distant.

"Aiden, please," I pleaded, desperation creeping into my voice. "Tell me something. How do you know Easton? Why did you say you were too late?"

He sighed, a battle raging within him. "I knew him a long time ago. We were once the closest of friends."

A chill ran down my spine. "What do you mean, 'once'? What happened?"

He hesitated, his expression grim. "I can't explain it all now. I need to get rid of this locket first."

"Why? What's so special about it?" I asked, my curiosity piqued.

He regarded me with a mixture of pity and warning. "It's a relic from a forgotten time. A time when dark forces threatened our world. It's connected to a power you don't fully understand. A power that could be dangerous if misused."

My heart pounded in my chest. "What kind of power?"

He hesitated, then spoke in a hushed tone. "A power that could make you a target for those who seek to control the world."

Fear gripped me. "What are you talking about? What do you mean?"

He sighed, his eyes filled with a profound sadness. "I can't explain it all now. But know this, Ember: I'll protect you, no matter what."

I stumbled backward, my knees buckling beneath me. The revelation hit me like a ton of bricks. "This can't be real," I whispered, disbelief etched on my face.

"It's true, Ember," he said, his voice heavy with sorrow. "We've lived countless lifetimes together, but each time, you've met an untimely end, just before your twenty-first year."

A cold dread settled over me. "But... my birthday is in a few months."

Panic flashed in his eyes. "That's why I need to destroy this locket. I can't lose you again."

"Aiden, wait!" I cried, fear gripping my heart. "What does Lucien want with me?"

"He desires your power, Ember," he explained, his voice low. "You're a unique soul, capable of great good or an even greater evil.

He seeks to control you, to bend you to his will."

"But why me? Why not someone else?" I asked, confusion clouding my mind.

"Because you're the key, Ember. The key to unlocking ancient power. He's been watching you, waiting for the right moment to strike."

A shiver ran down my spine. "I don't understand."

"You will," he promised, his voice filled with determination. "I won't let him hurt you."

The room spun, a whirlwind of fear and confusion. My blood ran cold and my face drained of color. Aiden's voice was a distant murmur, a whisper lost in the roar of my racing thoughts. His touch, once comforting, now felt distant, unreal. I was trapped in a nightmare, a prisoner of my own mind.

Panic seized me, a relentless storm that threatened to consume me. I couldn't breathe, couldn't think. The world narrowed down to a single, terrifying thought: the shadow man was real.

Then, his lips, warm and insistent, broke through the chaos. A jolt of electricity, a surge of primal instinct. His kiss, passionate and demanding, pulled me back from the abyss. Slowly, the storm began to subside. My heart rate slowed and my breathing steadied. The nightmare receded, replaced by the comforting reality of his embrace.

His gaze held mine, concern etched into his features. "Are you okay, love?" he asked, his voice gentle.

I tried to catch my breath, my heart still pounding in my chest. "How did you do that?" I managed to whisper, my voice barely audible.

He smiled, a look of relief washing over his face. "It's a little trick I learned," he said, picking me up and carrying me to the bed. "We'll deal with your abilities later. Right now, you need to rest."

"Don't leave me," I pleaded, my voice weak. "Please, stay with me."

He leaned down, his lips brushing mine. "I won't leave your side, my love. I promise."

The weight of sleep pulled at my eyelids, a relentless force I couldn't resist. I fought to stay awake, to hold onto the fading light of consciousness, but my efforts were futile. As darkness enveloped me, I tried to form the words, plead with Aiden to stay, to let me help. But my voice failed me, swallowed by the encroaching slumber. Was he somehow controlling my exhaustion, lulling me into a deep sleep? Lost in a haze of confusion, I succumbed to the darkness, leaving the unanswered questions hanging in the air.

Chapter Six

Sara's Surprise

I woke up late the following morning, rubbing the sleep from my eyes as I sat up in bed. Aiden was nowhere to be seen, but a note caught my attention on the nightstand. I sluggishly reached over to pick it up, finding a message from Aiden that read:

> *"My Love, I made sure that you would be safe, staying with you until sunrise. But it is important that I hide this locket and find out everything that Easton knows. I must protect you.*
>
> *I may be gone longer than expected, but please don't worry. I will be back and promise to explain everything when I return.*
>
> *Love, Aiden"*

His messy scrawl, a testament to his haste, only fueled my frustration. I yearned to be by his side, to unravel the mysteries he hinted at. My heart ached with longing, a longing that threatened to consume me. Perhaps he sensed my vulnerability, my inability to handle the truth, and decided to shield me from the darkness.

A restless energy surged through me, propelling me out of bed. A strange silence hung over the house, an eerie calm that unsettled me. My parents' bedroom door was opened, their snores muffled by the walls. They must have stayed out late, or perhaps they were simply sleeping in. I closed their door and tiptoed past their room, careful not to disturb their slumber.

The warmth of the shower enveloped me, washing away the tension and anxiety. As I stepped out, I heard a faint noise. A shuffling sound from the hallway. My parents must have woken up.

The clock ticked impatiently as I rushed to finish getting ready. My stomach grumbled, a persistent reminder of my neglected hunger. I hesitated, torn between avoiding my parents' inquisitive glances and succumbing to the gnawing hunger. In the end, my stomach won.

With a deep breath, I braced myself for the inevitable interrogation. As I stepped into the kitchen, I saw an unexpected sight: an empty house. My parents were gone, their whereabouts a mystery. A sense of relief washed over me, but it was quickly replaced by a growing curiosity. Where had they gone, and why so early?

I filled my plate with leftover breakfast, my mind still racing with questions. The quiet solitude of the house was both comforting and unsettling. I yearned to know what Aiden was up to, to ensure his safety.

The doorbell shattered the silence, interrupting my thoughts. Peering through the peephole, I saw Sara, her face lit up with excitement.

"Oh my gosh, Ember! You'll never guess what happened last night!" Sara burst through the door, her eyes wide with excitement. "I was walking home, and guess who I ran into?"

"Who?" I asked, taking a sip of my drink.

"Easton!"

I choked on my drink, my heart sinking. "Easton?" I repeated, incredulous.

"Yeah, Easton!" Sara exclaimed, oblivious to my discomfort. "He's back in town, and he wants to pick things up where we left off!"

"Oh, come on, Sara," I groaned. "You can't be serious."

"Why not?" she asked, defensively. "He seemed really sincere."

"But Sara, you know what happened last time. He disappeared without a trace. How can you trust him now?"

"I don't know," she admitted. "I was skeptical at first, too. But he said he's changed. That he wants to be honest with me. I told him I wouldn't tolerate any secrets or lies, and that I wouldn't keep anything from you. You're my best friend, after all."

"So, what did he say to all that?" I asked, raising an eyebrow. I was proud of her for standing her ground. But the words Aiden had spoken last night still lingered in my mind.

"He was a bit taken aback at first," Sara admitted. "He looked a little hurt, but I held firm. After a moment of silence, he finally agreed not to keep any more secrets from me, and he promised not to hide our relationship from you. I pressed him for details about where he'd been for the past three years, and he finally opened up."

My eyes widened in surprise. "And?"

"He said his parents got a divorce right after graduation. His dad moved to Florida, and his mom moved to California. He was left in a tough spot, with no money and nowhere to go. He didn't want to keep us hanging, so he broke things off."

That explanation is plausible, but why keep any of it a secret?... I thought to myself as Sara continued talking.

"So, first he lived with his dad in Florida, working odd jobs here and there. Then he had a falling out with his dad and moved to California to live with his mom. He got a decent job and saved up enough money to move back here," Sara said, her face glowing. "He couldn't stand being so far away, not knowing if I was okay.

"We walked around for a while after that, trying to keep the conversation going. It was a little awkward at first. I told him I'd mentioned our relationship to you, and he looked a bit surprised. We walked in silence for a few blocks.

"Then he grabbed my arm, and I swear, my heart almost stopped. It was a mix of excitement and fear. His voice was... different, kind of dark when he asked if I'd told you anything else. I got chills."

I felt a chill run down my spine too. "That's weird," I murmured. *Is he really not to be trusted?...* I thought to myself as Sara continued.

"I figured he may have been talking about our intimacy or I don't know, maybe that he was telepathic. But either way, I told him no."

My face grew hot from embarrassment as I let out a groan and whined. "Ahh… I wish I could forget that I had ever seen that!"

Sara giggled, unfazed by my embarrassment. "After that, he started telling me all about his life, how he was always moving around, never settling down. He said that's why he's so socially awkward, always being the new kid. Poor guy."

"Well, we started talking about lighter stuff, and then he grabbed my hand. I almost pulled away, but I let him. I know, I know, I shouldn't have, but he has a way of breaking down my defenses."

I forced a smile. "I didn't say anything about it, Sara." I was still a bit wary of Easton, remembering Aiden's warnings. I couldn't shake the feeling that he might be up to something, using Sara to get information about me.

"It felt like old times, you know? We were laughing, joking around, just being happy. But then, the guilt set in," Sara confessed, a shadow crossing her face. "That happiness, it was tainted. It felt bittersweet."

She paused, taking a deep breath. "I sat down on a bench, feeling overwhelmed. That's when Easton came and sat beside me, wiping away my tears. He tried to comfort me, but I just wanted to hide. I didn't want him to see how broken I was.

"He gently lifted my chin, forcing me to look at him. 'What's wrong, Sara?' he asked, his eyes filled with concern. I couldn't hide it anymore. I told him I was scared, scared to let him back in. I was terrified of getting hurt again, of being abandoned. I told him my heart was still broken, that it hadn't healed since he left. Being with him, made the emptiness even more painful." She chuckled, a bittersweet sound. "And of course, by that point, I was ugly crying."

"He just sat there, looking like a scolded puppy. I waited for him to say something, anything, but he was silent. I was so frustrated, so defeated. I turned to leave, feeling completely crushed."

"And then?" I asked, curious.

"Easton grabbed my wrist, his eyes filled with tears as he said, 'I'm so sorry, Sara. I left because I thought it was the best thing to do. I didn't want to drag you into a long-distance relationship. I wanted you to find someone better.' He said he came back to make sure I was happy, to make sure whoever I was with was treating me right."

Sara's eyes sparkled. "Can you believe it? He was so sincere. I believed every word."

I hesitated, not knowing how to break the news. "Sara..." I began, unsure of how to continue.

"Hm?"

"I want you to be happy, Sara," I said, my voice sincere. But the words Aiden had spoken echoed in my mind. What if Easton wasn't who he seemed? What if he was capable of hurting her? I was torn, unsure of what to do. Should I tell her about Aiden's warning? Or should I keep it to myself?

Sara held my hand, giving it a little squeeze. The gesture made me a little disoriented at first because she was only thinking of Easton, his face, and a whole collaboration of words that assaulted my mind, rendering me disoriented for a minute. She quickly withdrew her hand, realizing her mistake. "Sorry about that. I forgot I can't touch you," she explained with a giggle.

"You are very excited about things," I started after coming to my senses and getting up. "Jeez, you gave me a headache," I complained, trying to find some medicine.

Sara apologized before adding, "Oh, Ember, I am in such good spirits! Easton is going to take me out on a date tonight!" She gushed, practically clapping her hands together. "I asked him to walk me home after his speech and I thought over everything he had said. But my thoughts were interrupted when he decided to speak again. He said, 'Sara, I am going to be 100% honest with you from now on. I promise I will not disappear without giving you the truth. I know I broke your heart. It is something I regretted ever since I decided to do it.' Then he looked deeply into my eyes and said, 'I love you. I will never love another the way I do you. That day, I thought I was saving you, doing something good for you, but now… Now I realize that all I did was cause you an immense amount of pain and damage any attempt of you finding true happiness. If you won't take me back, I understand… If I was in your position, I wouldn't readily take someone back who hurt me so deeply. All I can do is tell you that I am being completely honest when I say I will never leave you or hurt you like that again. If it takes me the rest of my life to show you just how sorry I am and how much I love you, then that's what I'll do. I will spend every waking minute showing you how much I love you.'

"By the time he had finished, I knew I should be skeptical of his words. I know I shouldn't believe him so readily and keep him at bay, but I do believe him. When we reached my house, we gazed at each other for a few minutes before I worked up the courage to ask him to take me out to dinner. While I could tell Easton was surprised and excited by my question, I let him know real quick that this was a trial run."

She paused, lost in thought. "I told him that if we were going to make this work, we can't keep our relationship a secret from you. We need to start fresh, like we're new. We've both changed a lot in three years, and I need to get to know him again. He agreed to my terms, so we'll see how it goes."

I smiled at her, trying to be supportive. "Well, good luck, Sara. I hope it works out."

"So, did you sleep well last night?" Sara asked, changing the subject abruptly.

"Yeah... why?" I replied, a bit defensively.

Of course, my reaction tipped Sara off as she stared at me inquisitively. Her questioning gaze caused me to squirm as she replied, "I was just wondering if you slept all right. No dreams with the shadow man?"

"Oh," I replied, feeling a bit flustered. "No, no dreams about the shadow man."

Sara raised an eyebrow, her gaze piercing. "Well, that's good. You must be well-rested." She paused, then asked, "Would you like to come with me and Easton tonight?"

"No," I quickly replied. "It's a date. I don't want to be a third wheel." While I didn't want to intrude, I also didn't want to be around Easton, especially after what Aiden had said.

"Ember, something's up," Sara said, her voice firm. "You're being weird. Just tell me what's going on."

"What makes you think I'm hiding something?" I asked, trying to play it off.

"Come on, Ember," she said, her eyes narrowing. "You're acting strange. You never pass up an opportunity to get out of the house."

I sighed, knowing I couldn't keep up the act. "It's just... complicated," I mumbled.

"Why won't you tell me?" she asked, hurt.

I'm trying my best to sneak around the topic. With Easton's ability to look into Sara's mind, if I say anything about *him* or Aiden, then he will definitely know something is up. "I can't risk *someone* finding out."

She looked at me questioningly until it dawned on her that the "someone" I spoke of was Easton. "Then I'll pretend this conversation never happened and never think of it again."

"Sara, you know that doesn't work. Anytime people try to 'forget' something, that's all they think about. Other than that, it's obvious he can pick things out of anyone's head, even if it is long forgotten…"

Sadness filled her eyes as she said, "I guess I should just reschedule our date."

"No!" I exclaimed. "Sara, you should go. I'm happy for you. Don't let this weird stuff with me ruin your night."

"But you're my best friend," she protested.

"Please, go on your date," I insisted. "I'll figure out what to do. I don't want you to miss this chance."

"But something is going on with you and Easton, isn't there?" she asked, her eyes narrowing. "I want to know what's happening."

I sighed, feeling guilty. "It's complicated," I mumbled. "I just... I can't explain it right now."

"Well, you're going to have to explain it sooner or later," Sara said, her tone firm. "I'm not leaving until you tell me what's going on."

"Fine..." I replied with a defeated sigh before giving her a warning. "I can only tell you as much as I know and it isn't much at all. But after I say this, I don't know how long it will be until you can see Easton again. I can't risk him knowing anything that is happening because he is somehow a part of it."

"If that's the way it has to be, then that's how it's going to be."

I didn't respond because I was worried about what Aiden would say about me sharing this with Sara.

"Ember, you know I am in love with Easton. And if whatever you are going to say will jeopardize you or him, trust me, I will never utter another word. I will stay away from him if I have to."

Sara was adamant about cutting her losses with Easton, but her words were breaking her heart. She didn't want to do it and

I didn't want her to. But what am I supposed to do here??? "Sara, that's exactly what I don't want you to do. I know how you feel about him. Trust me I know, I experienced it firsthand. What you have with him is truly a blessing. But I just… I just don't have enough information on what I can say that would keep us safe… You see… he isn't the person to fear."

"Oh my gosh, Ember, just cut to the song already!" Sara demanded through her aggravation.

"Fine," I sighed, knowing I couldn't avoid it any longer. I told her everything Aiden had said last night: about Easton, Lucien, the locket, and their strange abilities. I even showed her the note Aiden had left this morning. "He's gone to get rid of the locket and find out more about Easton," I explained.

"Okay, Ember, I'm sorry, but are you sure this wasn't all just a dream?" Sara asked, her eyes wide with disbelief.

"It wasn't!" I insisted, feeling a bit defensive.

She pinched the bridge of her nose, looking frustrated. "Okay, Ember, I don't know what to believe. It's a lot to take in. Do you have any proof?"

I was taken aback by her skepticism. "What about this letter? You know this isn't my handwriting," I pointed out.

Sara's doubt was clear. She had always believed me in the past, no matter how strange the situation. But now, she seemed hesitant. It was as if she was questioning my sanity.

"I see the letter, Ember," Sara said, her voice cynical. "You know, I've always believed you, no matter how strange things got. But this... other realms, magic, special powers? It's a bit much, even for me."

I looked down, feeling a pang of hurt. I knew it sounded crazy, but I was telling the truth. "I know it sounds crazy," I admitted. "But it's real."

Sara sighed. "I'll reschedule my date with Easton. But Aiden needs to come back and explain everything." Seeing my pained expression, Sara's voice softened. "I'm not sure what to tell Easton, though."

"Just tell him I'm upset about something and need you..." I replied with hurt filling my voice, refusing to look at my friend.

Sara spent hours on the phone with Easton, leaving me alone with my thoughts. Was I being overly dramatic? Would I believe such a wild story if someone else told me? Either way, Sara insisted on staying the night, claiming she was worried about Lucien haunting my dreams. Whether she was genuinely concerned or had other motives, she was adamant about staying.

I couldn't shake the feeling that she was also curious about Aiden. She seemed eager to meet him, to see him for herself. But I knew he wouldn't be showing up tonight.

Soon, night fell, and we drifted off to sleep.

Chapter Seven
Journey to the Past

As I opened my eyes, I was greeted by a vibrant blue sky, the sun shining brightly overhead. I found myself lying in a vast open field, surrounded by trees that bordered a dense forest in the distance. Perched atop a small hill, I observed the tree line to the north and the forest behind me. My hair, half down and braided, cascaded over my shoulders, complementing the sheer, white summer dress that adorned my figure. Glancing down, I noticed my bare feet and hoped there were no thorns or stickers to contend with.

Taking in the serene landscape, my eyes settled on a charming cabin nestled in the center of the field, wisps of smoke curling from its chimney. Despite the smoke, the weather felt pleasantly warm, dispelling any notion of cold. The cabin, constructed from sturdy, aged wood, exuded a timeless strength that seemed capable of enduring for centuries.

As I strolled through the knee-high grass, I marveled at how it swayed gracefully in the gentle breeze. The field was dotted with flowers, each one adding a splash of color to the landscape - a rose here, a daffodil there.

My attention was suddenly drawn to a man standing at a distance from the house, his gaze fixed as if he were anticipating something. Intrigued, I started to make my way towards him when two magnificent horses came galloping past, frolicking as if engaged in a game of tag. I couldn't help but smile at the sight - I had never seen such beautiful horses before, let alone ones so playful.

One of the horses was predominantly white with tan markings on its legs, while the other resembled a dairy cow with its white coat adorned with black splotches. As they reached the cabin, they seemed to vanish into thin air, leaving me bewildered. How could such large creatures disappear into thin air? It was as if they had a magical ability to conceal themselves.

I glanced over at the man and continued to stride towards him, feeling a pang of disappointment as I noticed the horses were no longer in sight. Suddenly, I came to a halt when I realized who I was approaching.

"Aiden!" I exclaimed with excitement.

The man spun around, his face a mix of shock and joy. As he walked towards me, he enveloped me in a warm hug and planted a kiss on my cheek. "How did you get here?" he asked, clearly astonished.

"I'm not sure... I fell asleep and then suddenly found myself here," I replied, pausing to see his reaction. When he remained silent, I pressed on. "Is this all just a dream? Where exactly are we?"

"We are currently revisiting a memory, Ember. This is a place where we once lived," Aiden explained before our attention was diverted by a man and woman of our age fleeing from the house in opposite directions towards the forest. Fear gripped Aiden's expression before he turned back to me. "You shouldn't be here," he warned.

Confused, I gazed at him and asked, "But didn't you want me to remember?"

"No, I asked if you had any memories. I never said I wanted you to remember them! Some of them are..." He didn't finish his statement, becoming lost in thought.

As I walked towards the cabin, I asked, "So we used to live here?"

"Yes... And we were very happy, until that day," he replied sadly.

I gave Aiden a questioning look, but he wouldn't continue. "Did we have horses? How is it they disappeared?" I asked.

He finally smiled as he explained, "Those were our horses. Some things in memories, such as animals or objects, cannot stay focused in one's mind. For example, this is your first time remembering, so all the pieces may not be clear or they may disappear. Other times, if an animal or object disappears, it means you weren't paying much attention to them in the first place, so it would seem as though they just vanished."

We continued walking until we reached the southern tree line.

"We should turn back, my love," he said.

"Why?" I asked, puzzled by his reluctance.

"Because what lies beyond those trees is something you shouldn't see," he replied.

I gazed at the thick forest ahead, contemplating his words. "But shouldn't I be aware of what's happening?" I started to say, but when I turned to look at Aiden, he had vanished.

I stood still, scanning the vast countryside and calling out his name. After a few minutes of waiting, I decided to stay put and let him come back to me. It would be easier for him to find me where we last stood together.

As I waited, I sat cross-legged on the ground, absentmindedly twirling the grass between my fingers. Lost in contemplation, I was abruptly jolted from my thoughts by the sound of a branch snapping behind me. Whipping my head around, I was met with the sight of a deer gazing directly at me. "Hello," I greeted the creature tentatively, half-hoping for a response. Something was captivating about the deer. Compelling me to observe it more closely. Slowly rising, I asked, "What brings you out here?" A foolish question to pose to a deer, I realized as I cautiously approached it. However, before I could make any further attempts at communication, the deer bolted into the forest. "Wait!" I called out, as I chased it.

Upon entering the forest, the trees were sparse and widely spaced, but as I delved deeper, the foliage grew denser and the trees clustered closer together. The forest floor was blanketed with fallen leaves, and vegetation was scarce. I had lost track of time as I pursued the deer, but I was certain I had lost sight of it at least a mile back.

I paused beneath the towering branches of a massive oak tree, taking a moment to catch my breath and survey my surroundings. The trees stood like ancient sentinels, casting long shadows that blocked the sun's light and warmth. Despite the heat, I shivered as beads of sweat trickled down my exposed skin. Should I turn back, or press on? I pondered this question as I stood there, contemplating my next move.

As I weighed my options, I was startled by a sudden crunching sound that broke the silence. *Footsteps*, I realized, my heart racing as I instinctively ducked behind the tree for cover. The sound ceased on the other side, replaced by the heavy, labored breathing of an unseen presence.

I cautiously approached the massive oak tree, taking a few steps to catch a glimpse of the person standing on the other side. To my surprise, it was the same girl who had fled from the cabin earlier! She appeared to be around my age, with long brunette hair that matched my own. As she scanned the forest, searching for something or someone, her eyes met mine, but it was as if she didn't see me at all. Intrigued, I moved closer to her, studying her features in disbelief. To my shock, she bore a striking resemblance to me - from her long brunette hair and icy blue eyes to her nose and facial bone structure. The realization left me bewildered. What could possibly explain this uncanny resemblance?

"Ember!" A voice called out from behind me, causing both of us to turn and see who had called our names. To our surprise, it was

Aiden! However, he looked different from the last time I had seen him. His face appeared tired, and he had grown some facial hair that I found rather unappealing. Perhaps the beard was the fashion of the era we found ourselves in. It was uncanny how much Aiden and his Ember resembled us.

Aiden embraced his Ember, causing tears to well up in her eyes and cascade down her cheeks. "We must keep moving, my love," Aiden urged her.

She nodded in agreement, and they began to run. Intrigued, I followed closely behind, eager to discover what would unfold next. Deeper and deeper they ventured into the darkening woods until a thunderous voice stopped them in their tracks.

"Aiden," the disembodied voice began to laugh, "Do you truly believe that you can prevent the girl from reaching the King?" Suddenly, a man emerged from the shadows behind a tree. It was Easton!

Aiden gazed at his beloved Ember and urged her to flee. "No... I cannot leave without you!" she pleaded.

"I will find you, my love. Trust me. Now, go!" he replied firmly.

She kissed him, knowing it would be the last time, and then swiftly ran.

I stood there, torn between my past self and the new Aiden before me. Fortunately, the unfolding events quickly captured my attention and made the decision for me.

"Why do you defy the King's orders, Aiden? You were once one of his most trusted soldiers," Easton taunted with a sinister grin.

Aiden approached him calmly, ready to strike, but was suddenly restrained from behind by another man. Aiden was brought to his knees by the new figure, who held him firmly.

The man restraining Aiden had long, ethereal blonde hair that almost appeared white. His fair skin and piercing blue eyes seemed to see right through you, assessing and judging with a sharp gaze. Despite his slender frame, he effortlessly held Aiden in place. He was clad entirely in black, including a hooded flowing cape.

"You see, Aiden, allowing your emotions to cloud your judgment has made you vulnerable. *Your soulmate* is your weakness!" Easton taunted.

"I would rather be perceived as weak in your eyes than surrender her to Lucien! He is no king of mine!" Aiden retorted defiantly.

Easton simply chuckled at Aiden's response.

"Adam! I am surprised that you would support this!" Aiden addressed the man restraining him. "Would you truly hand Rosie over to Lucien?"

Adam's demeanor turned aggressive at Aiden's question, and he lashed out by punching him. "Never speak Rosie's name, you traitor!" he bellowed in anger.

Easton burst into a fit of laughter before exclaiming, "Look who's come to join the party!"

Ember, the newcomer, stood on the opposite side of the gathering, tears streaming down her face, her hair disheveled, and dirt smudged across her face. She cautiously made her way towards the crowd, with a woman looming behind her, holding a knife to her neck.

The woman had long, dark red hair, piercing green eyes, and pale skin. Her face bore a smirk that was infuriatingly smug. She stood slightly taller than me, dressed in all-black attire with a cape similar to her companions. Despite the apparent scuffle she and Ember had been in, the woman appeared unharmed.

I shifted my gaze away from the two newcomers in the group, turning to look at Aiden. His face had transformed from stern to furious as he witnessed his beloved in a dangerous and helpless situation. The intensity of his expression was almost demonic.

In a swift motion, Aiden swiftly struck Adam, snatching a knife from his boot and hurling it before Adam even hit the ground. Rosie, on the other hand, remained expressionless, her eyes fixed ahead. She dropped her knife to the ground, a throwing knife embedded in her forehead.

"Rosie!" Adam shouted as he ran towards her, cradling her in his arms as he saw the life fading from her eyes.

Ember saw an opening to escape towards Aiden, but Easton intercepted her.

"Release her!" Aiden commanded, his voice tinged with coldness. The transformation in his demeanor was striking, almost as if he had turned into a sociopath. His eyes darkened, his jaw clenched tightly as he locked eyes with Easton. "Let her go, Easton, NOW!"

"Do you honestly believe any of this would work?" Easton questioned, showing no concern for his friends lying on the ground, one of them dead. He glanced over at them and felt irritation creeping in. "Adam, quit your crying. We have a work to do."

As he finished speaking, more people appeared. A group of about five or six people encircled them.

"Aiden, did you truly believe you could conceal her? You are aware that the king would never allow you to keep her," one of the newcomers remarked.

Aiden took a step towards Easton and his Ember, causing the crowd to ready their weapons.

"The king will not be pleased to discover that you have slain one of his soldiers," Easton declared with a smirk.

Aiden only stared at him without making a sound, his eyes narrowed. I stood paralyzed as I observed Aiden in a new, slightly intimidating light. I could comprehend the reasons behind his behavior, yet I couldn't shake the fear that his gaze instilled in me, along with the unsettling aura he exuded.

Easton rested his head on Ember's shoulder, a sinister smile playing on his lips as he toyed with her hair. His gaze lingered on Aiden, a silent challenge in his eyes before he smoothly made his way over to the new arrival at the party. With a nonchalant air, he handed the now-restrained Ember off to another guest.

Continuing his calculated movements, Easton knelt beside Adam, placing a hand on his back. "I regret to inform you, Adam, that with your soulmate dead and the current state you find yourself in, your services are no longer needed." In one swift motion, he drew a knife and plunged it into Adam's chest and lung, leaving him gasping for breath on the ground next to Rosie.

Easton's behavior disgusted me. I never imagined he could be so heartless. "You're a monster!" Ember shouted, spitting at him. "I hope you suffer the same fate one day!"

He chuckled, "My dear girl, I will never find a soulmate! They hold you back," he said as he caressed her cheek. She recoiled from his touch, "They hinder you; preventing you from achieving your true potential."

"Hey, dumbass!" Aiden called out to Easton, interrupting him. "What were you saying?"

Easton's anger flared as he surveyed the aftermath left by Aiden. In a matter of moments, all the people Easton had brought with him were now incapacitated on the ground. The only ones left standing were Easton and the man holding Ember.

Before I could see what unfolded next, I felt a firm grip on my wrist, pulling me away. It was Aiden - my savior, the one who rescued me from the clutches of my shadowy tormentor.

"What is this?" I asked, my voice filled with disbelief.

"We must go," Aiden insisted urgently.

"No! I want to stay and see what happens!" I replied defiantly.

"We need to leave," Aiden demanded as he scooped me up and began to run away from the unfolding scene.

I glanced back at the four figures standing behind us, watching as they disappeared into the darkness. As we reached the edge of the forest, light began to filter through the trees.

My thoughts were abruptly interrupted by a piercing scream - my own scream - that echoed through the trees. A brilliant blue light suddenly caught my attention, emanating from the very spot where the unsettling scene had unfolded moments before. The light expanded rapidly, enveloping the entire forest before vanishing into thin air.

At that moment, Aiden set me down on the ground and proceeded to walk ahead, appearing visibly irritated with me.

"What was that, Aiden?" I asked, slightly shaken by the scream I had just heard. He remained silent, appearing to be lost in his thoughts as he continued walking. Unsure of how to get a response from him, I reluctantly trailed behind him, feeling defeated.

As we approached the field where the quaint cabin once stood, my heart sank at the sight of its current state - a mere shadow of its former self. The once charming structure now lay in ruins, with a gaping hole in its side and the wood decayed beyond repair. Some parts of the cabin appeared to have been ravaged by fire, while others were being slowly reclaimed by nature. I stood there, struck by the stark contrast between its previous beauty and its current devastation.

"What happened here?" I asked, turning to Aiden for answers.

"Ember, remember when I mentioned that this was a memory?" he began, his voice tinged with regret as I nodded in understanding. "This is just one of the many instances where I failed you..."

"It didn't look as though you had failed me back there," I reassured him, hoping to ease his guilt.

"Despite the battle to protect you and prevent you from falling into Lucien's hands, Easton still managed to capture you. The last thing you witnessed before Victor abducted you was Easton landing a lucky blow on me, causing me to collapse to the ground. The scream you heard was actually your own. That scream has haunted me ever since."

Tears welled up in my eyes as I struggled to comprehend the thought of Aiden being killed.

"The blue light you witnessed was him bringing you to Eternium," Easton explained.

I gazed at him in utter disbelief. *Why does everything suddenly seem so surreal?*

"How does that even create a light like that?" I questioned, then remembered the nightmare I had. "I saw a red light in my nightmare! It appeared right after Sara was murdered."

A sense of unease washed over Aiden before he spoke, "Eternium exists in a separate realm from our own. They possess the ability to travel effortlessly. You and I require a specific object to travel. When Eternium beings move, a distinctive light is visible... I once had the ability to travel freely..."

"You can't anymore?"

"No."

"Why not? What happened?"

"That is a story for a different time." He stated.

"Why did you suddenly disappear earlier, before I entered the forest?" I asked.

Aiden flashed his charming smile before replying, "I woke up." His simple answer made me smile in return. "It took me some time to return here because it's difficult to rest where I am sleeping."

"Where exactly are you sleeping?" I questioned with concern.

"Not far from you." He stated simply.

I glared at him. "How do I know that you are telling me the truth? How do I know that none of this is just a dream that I made up?"

"I guess you don't, my love."

Chapter Eight

The Unexpected Visitor

It has been almost a week since I had that dream and seen Aiden. I did not tell Sara about the dream or memory that I had because I could not risk Easton finding out. What if it was all just a dream? I couldn't belittle Easton's character which may not have occurred. Plus I didn't want to sully Sara and her boyfriend's reconciliation. She was absolutely smitten with him.

Sara waited with me for a couple of days for Aiden to return but to no avail. After growing tired of the wait, she made plans with Easton and they have been going on many dates. I haven't seen so little of my best friend since we were younger and had to rely on our parents to bring us everywhere. It's not her fault though. She has invited me to hang out with them a few times, but I can't look at Easton the same way since that dream.

I started to question Aiden's existence. Was he real, or just a figment of my imagination? Even with my doubts, I couldn't stop worrying about him. The dreams of him and Lucien had stopped, the visions had faded. Was it possible that my telepathy had driven me mad?

A knock at the door startled me from my thoughts. I rushed to the door, heart pounding. My mom must be home early, I thought. But when I opened the door, I saw an unexpected sight.

"Will!" I exclaimed, surprised to see my brother.

"Hey, little sis," he grinned, pulling me into a hug. "I was knocking at the front door. Didn't you hear it?"

"No, I guess I was too lost in thought," I admitted, still a bit dazed. "What are you doing here?"

"I have some news," he said mysteriously.

"What kind of news?" I asked, intrigued.

"You'll have to wait," he replied. "I'll tell you when Mom and Dad get home."

I gave him a pout.

He chuckled. "Do you want to get out of the house for a while?"

I didn't respond. I grabbed my coat and boots and was out the door with my brother. We walked silently for a couple of blocks as Will appeared deep in thought.

The silence was driving me crazy. "So who is she and when is the wedding?"

Will stared at me completely dumbfounded. "How did you know?"

"Lucky guess," I said with a smile.

"Right... Well, you hit the nail on the head with that one," he replied, a hint of annoyance in his voice.

"Well, it was either that or you knocked someone up. That was my next guess," I teased.

"Oh, ha-ha," he retorted. "Anyway, her name is Cindy. We've been together for about nine months, and she's amazing!"

"I'm happy for you, Will," I said sincerely.

"So, would you like to meet her?" he asked hopefully. "I thought it would be better if you met her first, so Mom and Dad wouldn't scare her off."

I laughed nervously. "Sure, I guess. When?"

"A little later today," he replied hopeful.

"Alright." I sighed inwardly. I wasn't exactly in the mood to meet new people, especially when I felt overwhelmed.

Will gave me a look of confusion, but brushed it away before asking, "What have you been up to? Any boyfriend I should know about?"

"Not really... There's this guy I met a week or so ago that I thought could work out, but he kind of just disappeared."

"Do I need to kick his ass?" he asked defensively.

I laughed sheepishly. "No... It's nothing to worry about." I lied. This was a topic that I did not feel like touching. "Besides, if I wanted you to, I wouldn't know where to find him; hence the term 'disappeared.'"

"You know, I did miss your smart ass," he said sarcastically. "How's Sara doing?"

"She's fine... In love with some guy from high school," I replied.

"Who's that?" he asked, though I doubted he cared much.

"Easton," I answered.

"Never heard of him," he said.

"Yeah, he was kind of a loner," I explained.

"Do you like him?" he asked.

"I don't know," I admitted. "I hardly know him." I wasn't really in the mood to discuss my love life.

"Well, you should get to know him," he suggested. "He *is* dating your best friend, after all."

"Yeah, but I have my own stuff to deal with right now."

We strolled through town, catching up on lost time. Will had landed a job in construction. After an accident at work, he had to pick up some medicine at a pharmacy, where he met his fiancée, Cindy. According to Will, he didn't have to try very hard to get her to go out with him. I highly doubted this and as he told me the story, the real scene played out in my head as he recollected the moment.

Cindy was a beautiful girl, about my height with long straight black hair. She had brown eyes and tan skin. It was apparent that she had some type of Native American in her, especially with her high cheekbones.

Will had walked up to her and handed her his prescription. She looked at him sheepishly and gave him a cute smile as she went to fill it. When she came back he had asked her for her phone number, which she declined to give to him. Then he asked her out on a date, to which she replied no. He went up there every day until she said yes. It was kind of funny to think about, especially since he lied about how easy it was for him to go on a date with her. It was quite shocking that she didn't call the cops claiming he was a stalker.

At about four o'clock in the afternoon, Will took me to the park where Cindy was waiting to meet us. She was sitting on a bench by herself reading a magazine.

"Cindy," Will began, "this is my sister, Ember."

Her eyes met mine, a lazy smile playing on her lips. "Hello," she murmured.

"It's nice to meet you," I replied, returning her smile.

She seemed a bit distracted, lost in her own thoughts. Perhaps she was nervous, but her lack of effort in making a good first impression was puzzling.

"So, Will told me he swept you off your feet," I ventured.

She giggled, finally showing some life. "Hardly. He practically stalked me until I agreed to go out with him. I told him I'd only go if he stopped coming to the pharmacy. It wasn't exactly romantic... It wasn't something I would have normally done but he seemed harmless."

Will flushed, caught in his own lie.

We chatted for another hour, but the conversation was stilted. Her mind seemed to wander constantly, making it hard to keep up. I couldn't help but feel a bit disconnected from her.

Once we finished talking, Will walked with me to get my opinion.

"So what did you think of her?" His voice was hopeful.

"She didn't seem very sociable." To be honest, from this meeting, I couldn't see what Will saw in her. Hopefully, I would find it soon because he cared for her a lot.

"She was just nervous…" His voice trailed off. "Do you think Mom and Dad will like her?"

"I think you should spend some time with them before springing this on them," I replied, thoughtfully. "It's not that they would disapprove; it's just, I think there has been a lot of excitement this past week and you know how mom is…"

"Does she still have those mood swings?" Will asked, a hint of disdain in his voice.

"Something like that," I replied, a bit uncomfortable.

"Some things never change, I guess," he muttered.

As we walked home, I spotted Easton walking towards us. I prayed he wouldn't see me, but of course, he did.

"Hey, Ember," he greeted, a familiar smile on his face. "Haven't seen you in ages. What's new?"

"Oh, nothing... I just haven't been feeling very well... I've been going through some things..." I paused, trying to think of something else besides the disgusting vision of him from that night... but I simply couldn't. I wanted to get as far away from him as possible. The silence that once gave me comfort now made me feel threatened, weak, and defenseless.

Easton gave a pained expression for a split second before recovering his jovial facade.

"So... Where is Sara?" I asked concerned because she has been with him every day and night this past week.

"She's at work," he replied with a smile before looking at my brother. "Hello," he greeted as he extended his hand out to shake Will's, "I'm Easton."

Will returned a smile, "Will. It's nice to meet you."

"Well, Ember never told me she had a brother."

"Is that right?" Will looked at me teasingly with a sad face.

I shrugged my shoulders. "Never came up. Easton is a private person and we never conversed much in high school," I replied defensively.

Easton's smile faded before returning; strained. "Well... I must go pick up Sara." He said goodbye to Will and then looked me dead in the eye. "Hopefully we will see you sometime soon."

"Yeah..." I said slowly, trying not to allow my true feelings to show, which was unsuccessful.

He gave me an odd look filled with regret, guilt, and pain. "See you later..." his voice was filled with melancholy.

Will and I started walking back to the house without speaking again. There was a lot of tension coming from Will as he thought of meeting Mom and Dad for the first time in over a year.

"Calm down, I can feel your anxiety from here."

"Sorry."

We turned the corner and saw our parents' car in the driveway. Will hesitated, a look of uncertainty on his face.

I looked at him questioningly. *Is he really that anxious about seeing Mom and Dad?*

"Should we go in?" He asked nervously.

"I don't know about you, but I'll have to eventually," I replied, rolling my eyes playfully. Will skittishly followed behind me. Noticing his demeanor as I walked in, I turned to him and said quietly, "You're being a child! You are getting married soon, so act like a man for Pete's sake!" He looked at me sternly before fixing his posture, standing tall and gaining courage.

As we filed in, we noticed Dad sitting in his recliner watching TV as my mom made dinner in the kitchen. Will and I gave each other a blank look.

"Mom, look who I found," I announced.

She turned around and almost fell to the floor. "Will…"

"Hi." He said awkwardly with a fake smile.

My dad entered the room and grunted before saying, "Where have you been hiding, boy?"

*****

The dinner conversation dragged on, focused on Will's life, his job, and his fiancée. My parents were genuinely interested, peppering him with questions. I sat through the meal, lost in my thoughts, barely touching my food.

Just as I was starting to feel restless, Sara walked through the door. Her eyes widened in surprise when she saw Will. "Hey," she greeted him, a blush creeping onto her cheeks.

"Hello," Will replied, a knowing smile playing on his lips. "I hear you've got a serious boyfriend."

Sara blushed again. "Yeah..."

"That's good," Will said, turning back to my parents.

I excused myself and led Sara to my room.

"Why didn't you tell me your brother was back?" Sara asked, closing the door behind her.

"He just showed up a few hours ago," I replied.

"What happened?" she asked, expecting some dramatic reason for his return.

"Nothing. He's just getting married," I explained.

"Oh my God! When?" she exclaimed, excited.

"He didn't say," I replied, sitting on my bed.

"You don't seem very excited," she observed. "Is she a bitch or something?"

"No, not a bitch," I chuckled. "She's just. Kind of spaced out, always thinking about something else. She doesn't seem too interested in anything. Everything just seemed to be boring to her." I shrugged my shoulders. "I'm hoping she was just nervous."

Sara nodded, understanding.

"So, what have you come to tell me?"

"We haven't seen each other in a few days," Sara said, confused. "I thought we could hang out."

"Did you get tired of Easton already?" I asked, a bit too sharply.

"What do you mean by that?" Sara asked, her tone defensive.

"Nothing," I muttered. "I'm just in a bad mood."

"Why?" she pressed.

"Because everyone is smiling, laughing, and sharing stories as if nothing ever happened! Will was gone over a year, no one knew if he was dead or alive, he never wrote or called to see if I, Mom, or Dad was ok." I started a rant and kept going with it, laying all of my frustrations out on the table. "On top of that, I can't even discuss with you other things because it deals with Easton. But above all, I feel like I am going insane because I may or may not have made Aiden up in my mind! He hasn't called or tried to get in touch with me whatsoever!"

Sara stared at me, a mix of anger and concern on her face. "You're not going crazy," she said firmly. "I saw Aiden at the diner. And your family is just being your family."

"I think I just need to be alone," I snapped, feeling overwhelmed.

"I think you've spent enough time alone." She countered. "You wouldn't be this agitated if you had someone with you, someone to talk to."

"Just go hang out with Easton," I retorted, anger clouding my judgment. "That's what you really want to do anyway."

Sara looked hurt, her eyes welling up with tears. Without a word, she gathered her things and left.

I felt terrible about how I'd treated Sara. I knew I'd been harsh and unfair. I sulked in my room, replaying the argument in my head.

A couple of hours later, Will announced he was going to meet Cindy. As he left, I went outside to say goodbye. When I returned to my room, I was shocked to see Aiden sitting on my bed, a wide grin on his face.

"Happy to see me?" he asked.

I slammed the door shut and glared at him. "Where have you been?" I demanded.

"I've been doing what I said I would," he replied calmly. "Spying on Easton."

"You need to explain yourself, and you need to explain it now!" I yelled, frustration boiling over. "I've been worried sick, thinking I was losing my mind! I've been avoiding Sara and Easton, isolating myself, all because of you!"

The smile faded from Aiden's face as I recounted the chaos he'd caused. "I'm sorry, my love," he apologized. "I never meant to make you doubt yourself. But finding you this time was more difficult than usual." He sighed, his expression troubled. "It would be easier to just show you."

He moved closer, taking my hands in his. "Just breathe, love. You might feel a bit disoriented at first, but it'll all make sense soon enough."

I pulled my hands away, confusion etched on my face. "What are you doing?" I asked, wary.

"Showing you everything," he replied, his eyes intense. "From the beginning."

Chapter Nine

Eternium

Aiden opened his mind, allowing me into his memories, and inviting me to step through. I found myself in a world unlike any I'd ever imagined. It was a medieval city, yet infused with advanced technology. Stone buildings towered over cobblestone streets, while quaint cottages dotted the outskirts. The sky was a mesmerizing blend of deep blue and purple, illuminated by two luminous moons. The very trees and plants seemed to glow with an ethereal light. Eternium was a breathtaking sight, a place of wonder and mystery.

I was awestruck, then I could hear Aiden's voice ringing in my ears.

"Everyone here is telepathic. Many believe the gift came from our ancestors, bestowed on us from godly forces. Others assume it has something to do with the moons or minerals in the soil. Either way, it's a gift that requires constant vigilance. We must learn to

shield our minds, to keep our deepest thoughts private. A single slip, a moment of weakness, could expose our innermost secrets to the world.

"This world, Eternium, is unlike any other. Here, telepathy is just the beginning. Some possess extraordinary abilities, bending reality to their will. Others can traverse dimensions, crossing the boundaries of space and time. And for some, there's a unique connection, a soulmate bond that draws them together across the cosmos. Though many possess this ability, finding one's true match is a rare and precious gift."

I watched the scene unfold like a play. The city bustled with activity. People worked, children played, and everyone seemed to have a purpose. There was no need for money in Eternium as skills and passions were valued. A talented fighter joined the king's guard, a skilled hunter provided food for the community, and a gifted architect designed stunning buildings. Those who contributed were rewarded with everything they needed. Those who didn't help in some way were left to fend for themselves.

As night fell, the city transformed into a vibrant, festive place. The streets were illuminated, fireworks lit up the sky, and countless feasts were laid out. The people danced, sang, and celebrated, their spirits lifted by the communal joy. Of course, the king's guard stood watch, ensuring peace and order amidst the revelry.

The imposing royal castle loomed over the city, home to the benevolent king and queen. Chosen from birth, they were raised to rule with compassion and wisdom. King Aldrich, a kind and gentle soul with a warm smile and a flowing beard, hosted nightly dinners for his people, whom he preferred to call his fellow townsfolk.

Queen Sophie, a vision of grace and beauty, complemented her husband perfectly. Their children, Prince Cadeyrn and Princess Amara were raised to be just as compassionate. The prince, a bright-eyed boy of ten, inherited his father's kind nature. The princess, a delicate seven-year-old, was a spitting image of her mother.

The grand dining hall awaited, a cavernous space with stone walls adorned with roaring fireplaces. Long wooden tables, each capable of seating fifty, stretched across the room. The high, narrow windows bathed the hall in soft, natural light during the day, while at night, the gentle glow of gas lanterns created a warm and inviting atmosphere.

Aiden was a natural warrior, a rising star in the king's guard. His prowess in hand-to-hand combat and his skill with weapons, from swords to throwing knives, made him a force to be reckoned with. He quickly rose through the ranks, becoming second in command. Easton, his fellow trainee, proved to be a formidable rival, pushing Aiden to be even better.

"We shared many of the same interests and would often compete with one another for fun. Aiden's voice rang in my ears again. *We constantly made each other better this way, excelling quicker."*

The scene changed from a completely magical place to a courtyard with training dummies and targets. There was a man that Aiden was particularly focused on. The man was scrawny, not one that you would necessarily expect to be training with the king's guard. He looked peculiar, and everyone seemed to think him odd because everyone was staring at him. A little blush washed over his face as he realized everyone was staring at him.

"One day, Easton and I were training new recruits when Lucien showed up. He was... underwhelming, to say the least. But then, he unleashed a telepathic power that stunned us all. It was unlike anything we'd ever seen."

A narrow staircase led from the dining hall to the soldiers' barracks, a long, dimly lit room lined with cots and personal chests. Beyond the barracks, a hidden door led to a secluded courtyard, a training ground shielded from the eyes of the outside world.

Beneath the castle, a winding staircase descended into a series of dank, dimly lit cells. These were rarely used, reserved for those who broke the law or acted out of line during drunken revelry.

To the left of the dining hall, a stone staircase led to the servants' quarters. Maids, cooks, and royal attendants inhabited the numerous rooms along the corridor. A vast library, its shelves reaching from floor to ceiling, lined one side of the hall.

Beyond the library, another staircase led to the private quarters of the royal family. There were rooms for the king and queen, a study, a playroom for the children, and several guest rooms. A secret passageway led to a secluded garden, a tranquil retreat for the royal family. Few were granted access to this private sanctuary.

The castle was a masterpiece of opulence, adorned with rich tapestries and exquisite vases filled with vibrant flowers. The grand foyer displayed a collection of ancestral relics, a testament to the family's rich history. Portraits of noble ancestors, brave soldiers, and breathtaking landscapes lined the corridors.

"I reported the trainee's performance to King Aldrich, who was intrigued by Lucien's potential. While his combat skills were lacking, his telepathic abilities could be invaluable, especially in times of war. The king wasn't exactly sure how to utilize Lucien's power, but he recognized its potential." My heart sank as I

realized the identity of the unassuming young man.

Lucien, as Aiden remembered him, was not traditionally handsome. He stood at 5'5", with deep blue eyes and light brown hair streaked with silver which was pulled back to show his slender face.

"Lucien was an enigma, a solitary figure who often retreated to the library. He spent countless hours immersed in books, exploring realms of knowledge from history to architecture, even delving into the art of cooking. His quiet nature often made him seem aloof, but he was never excluded from the camaraderie of the guard."

The scene shifted abruptly, no longer focusing on Lucien's quiet study. Instead, I found myself in a grand room, a fire crackling in the hearth. The King sat, with a look of concern etched on his face, as Easton and Aiden stood opposite.

"About a year or two later, Easton and I were called on by King Aldrich. We stood before him in his study awaiting our orders." Aiden's voice echoed once more.

"I know both of you have been observing Lucien," the King began, his voice low. "Have you noticed anything unusual, any plans he might be making?" His eyes, sharp and intense, scanned their faces.

"No, sir," Aiden replied, his brow furrowed.

"No, sir," Easton echoed, equally puzzled.

The King leaned back, a sigh of relief escaping his lips. "Good, good. It seems you two are not involved. However, I need you to find Lucien. He's gone to stay with his aunt in a cottage outside the city. Bring him back to me. We must ensure he doesn't cause any harm."

Aiden's confusion deepened. "Sir, what has he done? What are we accusing him of?" he asked.

The king turned around fighting to hold back rage at Aiden's inquiries. "Treason..." he finally stated with his jaw clenched. "Now bring him to my quarters immediately!"

"Yes, sir!" Easton and Aiden answered in unison.

They walked down the corridor, down the first flight of stairs, then the next until they were out of the castle. Both men wanted to be away from the king before they started talking.

Aiden and Easton exchanged a confused glance. "Treason?" Easton echoed. "What could he have possibly done?"

Aiden shrugged. "I don't know, but the king wouldn't accuse him without reason. Someone must have been watching him."

As they walked through the dimly lit streets, Easton's skepticism grew. "We see him every day. He seems perfectly normal. How could he be a traitor?" His face betrayed his emotion as he fought not to question the king's motives.

Aiden remained silent, his mind racing. They walked side by side down the dark streets that were starting to fill with residents partying. The trees illuminated the streets with a green glow while the gas lamps made the visibility better. When the group of people started to become more spread out as they walked past the party, Easton began again, "Do you think it could be possible that the king may be going senile?"

Aiden shrugged. "I don't think he's that old."

"But what could he have done to be accused of treason?" Easton pressed.

Aiden shook his head. "I don't know."

He must have lived deep in the woods because soon they weren't walking on a path anymore. If there was one, then it was overgrown and not well managed by those who lived out here.

"Most of the people this far out of the way usually do not contribute to the town. They mostly want to stay to themselves; not be bothered." Aiden's invasive voice explained.

Nestled deep within the forest, obscured by overgrown weeds and plants, stood a quaint, diminutive cottage. The surrounding trees were barren, devoid of any signs of life or magic, casting a somber shadow over the dwelling. The cabin itself seemed too small to accommodate more than one person, with a front door positioned in the center of its rectangular facade, flanked by two windows. A set of narrow, uneven stairs led up to the entrance, making it clear that only one person could ascend at a time. Despite its modest size, it appeared that as many as five people called this mysterious cottage home.

Aiden ascended the rickety steps, knocking on the door. They waited in silence, the only sound the creak of the opening door.

"Yes?" a monotonous voice greeted them.

"Lucien, we've been sent by the king," Aiden said, his voice stern. "You're under arrest for treason."

Lucien's expression turned sour. "Treason, huh?" he scoffed, closing the door behind him. "Let's go, then."

"We just need to bring you in for questioning," Easton interjected, trying to ease the tension. "Maybe we can get this sorted out quickly."

Lucien only laughed at Easton's lament. "You two are complete fools. If the 'king'" he said with disgust, "wishes to see me, then he only need come."

Aiden and Easton were taken aback by this statement.

"You know that's not how this works..." Easton replied.

"Lucien, come peacefully or we are authorized to use force," Aiden stated.

"I'd love to see you try." A smirk of amusement spread across his face.

Aiden's anger flared as Lucien's defiant words hung in the air. Suddenly, Lucien doubled over, clutching his head in pain. A silent battle raged between the two, a battle of wills played out through telepathic force.

"Aiden, that's enough," Easton warned, restraining Lucien. "Stop!"

Aiden's gaze remained locked on Lucien, his expression hard and unforgiving.

"Don't ever challenge me," he growled, his voice low and menacing.

Lucien lay on the ground, his laughter echoing in the air as his hands were bound. Easton, concerned, helped him to his feet and scolded Aiden for his actions.

"Geeze Aiden, that was unnecessary. You could have killed him! What exactly did you do?" Easton demanded, his voice filled with anger.

Aiden, unfazed, explained his method calmly. "I simply overloaded his mind with a barrage of images and high-frequency sounds. It may seem extreme, but it made our jobs a whole hell of a lot easier."

The trio returned to the lively town, with Lucien laughing uncontrollably the entire journey. His laughter did not cease even when they stood before the imposing figure of King Aldrich.

"What is this?" King Aldrich demanded, pointing towards the giggling Lucien who knelt before him.

"It appears that Aiden may have taken the 'lethal force' order a bit too far," Easton replied a hint of amusement in his voice.

The king grunted before asking Easton to leave. "Aiden, you wait by the door. I have questions for this man, but I think he may be staying in the dungeons tonight."

Aiden obeyed his order, only able to hear murmurs of the king's voice and the hysterical laughter from Lucien. After a few minutes, the king's voice became louder as rage began to fill within him. His words became indistinguishable and he began to speak quickly. "Aiden!" The king finally yelled for him to enter the room. "Bring this fool to the dungeon where he may rot until he loosens his lips!"

This statement shocked Aiden. "Yes, sir." He replied with a sense of trouble.

"The king was furious, but even at his most cross, he would never make you suffer."

"You are no king! You are nothing but a traitor, Aldrich!" Lucien screamed as Aiden lifted him to his feet. "The truth lies in the other realms! Your reign is meaningless!"

"Wait, Aiden!" the king commanded as he approached Lucien. Placing his thumbs on Lucien's forehead and his fingers around the back of his head, a blinding flash of white light filled the room. Lucien now lay unconscious on the floor, defeated by the power of the king.

"The king stripped Lucien of his ability to traverse different realms. An ability that only a royal family member is allowed to have. King Aldrich had never before utilized this ability, as few monarchs had ever needed to do so. Only one king before him had wielded this power against a subject.

"Despite King Alrich's remorse for taking away this power, he knew it was a necessary action. The weight of his decision hung heavy upon his shoulders, but duty demanded sacrifice.

"For weeks on end, Lucien languished in the dark, damp dungeons, steadfastly refusing to provide the king with the information he sought. Each passing week, the king stripped away another of Lucien's powers, holding out

the promise of their return should he choose to cooperate. But Lucien remained resolute until all that remained was his telepathy - a gift inherent to all beings.

"The king, recognizing the gravity of taking away such a fundamental ability, spared Lucien's telepathy. To do otherwise would be akin to snuffing out his very essence. Little did the king know, this decision would have dire repercussions.

"The consequences of the king's choice would soon unfold, casting a shadow over the kingdom and forever altering the course of history."

As Aiden spoke to me, I watched a mirage of Lucien day after day in the dungeons, refusing to eat his meals. He had become paranoid, verging on insane.

"I was tasked with the duty of watching over him on multiple occasions, each time witnessing his gradual deterioration. As the days passed, a sense of unease settled over Eternium. The once lively streets were now filled with heated arguments, and the joyous parties had devolved into violent brawls.

"The very people we had sworn to protect had turned against us, their trust eroded by whispers of discontent. Even with Lucien imprisoned beneath the castle, his malevolent influence seeped into the hearts of the populace. He sowed seeds of doubt and fear, painting the king as a tyrant and a traitor.

"The once harmonious kingdom now teetered on the brink of chaos, with rebellion simmering just beneath the surface. Our once beloved ruler was now viewed with suspicion and scorn, his authority undermined by the insidious machinations of a single man. The shadows of treachery and deceit loomed large over Eternium, threatening to plunge us into darkness."

The scene shifted to reveal that weeks had passed, and the chambers were now filled with a multitude of feeble-minded individuals. Among them were acquaintances of Aiden and fellow guardsmen who had made a futile attempt on the king's life. Everyone began losing hope.

"The townsfolk united in a fierce resistance against the rebels spawned by

Lucien. Some were recruited as guardsmen, while others turned rogue due to their unsuitability for the role.

"The collapse of our society unfolded before my eyes with each passing hour of Lucien's imprisonment. King Aldrich attempted to reason with him, begging for an end to the chaos, only to be met with mocking laughter from Lucien.

"As time passed, we received word of a sinister plot. A horde of townspeople planned to storm the castle that night, intent on freeing Lucien and slaying the royal family. Every guardsman was summoned to defend against the impending threat. We couldn't risk escalating the situation by resorting to violence or interrogation, as it would only validate Lucien's corruption. So we stood ready, bracing for the inevitable clash.

"What unfolded that night was beyond anything I could have imagined..."

"Aiden, go fight with your comrades. I shall stay here in my chamber... Stay with them, protect them, but try not to die." The king ordered.

"I found this request to be odd. The king never just stayed in his quarters in a time of war. He was always there fighting alongside his men to personally resolve the issue at hand."

"But sir," Aiden began, his voice filled with conviction, "I believe my skills are better suited to serve your needs."

The king, his expression tinged with sadness, replied with a gentle smile, "Go now, Aiden. Protect your people."

Aiden, though burdened by a heavy heart, obeyed the king's command, sensing that something ominous loomed on the horizon. As he turned to leave, the king spoke in a wistful tone, "You have always been a valiant warrior, Aiden. A true friend and a fiercely loyal guardian. I am grateful to have a man like you by my side." With those words, the king closed the door, cutting off any further conversation.

Aiden felt a surge of anger rising within him, torn between his duty to protect the king and the need to assist his comrades in holding back the rioting townspeople. The weight of his decision pressed heavily upon him, knowing he could not be in two places at once.

Lost in his thoughts, Aiden suddenly noticed Easton approaching. "Easton," he called out, his voice commanding, "Guard the king's door. Keep watch for any angry villagers attempting to breach our defenses."

"But I am meant to stay up high," Easton protested. His orders were to use his archery skills to keep the enemy at bay. "I am tasked with keeping them at a distance."

The tension in the air was palpable as Aiden and Easton stood at a crossroads, each facing their own challenges amid turmoil and uncertainty.

"Well, your orders have changed," Aiden declared icily, his intense gaze locking onto Easton's eyes.

"Alright, man," Easton responded, confusion clouding his features. "Just stay calm, dude."

Easton made his way to his new post, while Aiden descended the stairwells until he reached the dining hall entrance. The once vibrant city now appeared desolate and ominous. Soldiers stood guard at the castle's gate, their weapons at the ready. Archers were positioned on the rooftops and other elevated areas, arrows aimed at potential invaders.

A furious mob gathered twelve feet away, brandishing makeshift weapons and torches. The air was filled with their deafening screams and chants, directed at the soldiers. The chaotic cacophony of voices made it impossible to discern their words, adding to the tension and uncertainty of the situation.

Aiden stood proudly before the soldiers, his voice unwavering as he addressed them. "We are here to maintain peace and protect the castle and the royal family. We will not allow these misguided citizens to breach our defenses." His words echoed with authority, commanding the attention of the soldiers before him. "We have been given orders to use force if necessary, but only as a last resort. Your safety and the safety of your comrades is our top priority. Do you understand our orders?"

"Yes, sir!" the soldiers responded in unison, their voices filled with determination.

As the soldiers stood ready, the tension in the air was palpable. Suddenly, the rioters made their move, charging towards the castle in a wave of chaos. The soldiers were outnumbered, but Aiden's courage shone through as he fought alongside his comrades, taking down the criminals one by one.

Amidst the chaos, a commotion erupted from within the castle, breaking Aiden's focus. Without hesitation, he left his fellow soldiers behind, determined to discover the source of the disturbance. The fate of the castle and the royal family hung in the balance, and Aiden was ready to face whatever challenges lay ahead.

Chaos reigned within the castle walls as prisoners ran amok, leaving destruction in their wake. The once grand dining hall was now a scene of devastation, with flames licking at the furniture and the very walls themselves. The stairwells leading to the king's chambers had been pillaged, priceless paintings torn to shreds, and the hallway resembled a war zone with debris and missing chunks of stone scattered about.

Aiden raced towards the king's chambers, his heart pounding in his chest. As he approached the door, he could hear muffled voices from within. With weapon in hand, he burst through the door, ready to confront whatever lay on the other side.

"Release the king!" Aiden demanded, his eyes blazing with fury as he waited for Lucien to comply.

The king knelt on the ground, his arms bound behind his back, tears streaming down his face. He locked eyes with Aiden and gave a subtle nod before his life was cruelly taken in a matter of moments.

"No!" Aiden cried out, rushing to the side of the dying king.

Lucien stood by, a sinister smile playing on his lips as he reveled in the success of his treacherous scheme.

Aiden cradled the king in his arms, watching helplessly as the light faded from his eyes. King Aldrich weakly motioned for Aiden to come closer, his final moments filled with a sense of urgency and unspoken words.

He obeyed, moving his ear to the king's mouth.

In his last breath, he whispered, "Follow him… Even if he is not worth it… Follow his leadership and then you can find yourself where you belong and… take… him.. down…" A gasp left the king's body and he now lies motionless on the floor.

"After this day… everything in Eternium had changed…"

Chapter Ten

Aftermath

Aiden's eyes blazed with fury as he glared at Lucien, who was still cackling maniacally. Easton emerged from the shadows, his face a mask of conflicting emotions.

"Easton, kill him!" Aiden commanded, his voice filled with rage.

But Easton hesitated, a flicker of guilt in his eyes.

Aiden's heart pounded in his chest as he realized the truth. His once-trusted friend had betrayed him and their kingdom. He lunged forward, ready to strike, but an unseen force held him back. His body refused to move, his muscles locked in place.

Lucien's laughter echoed through the cottage, a chilling sound. "Do you really think you can break through my defenses?" he taunted. "Aldrich was right about you. A loyal fool, to the end."

Aiden's anger flared. "Don't speak ill of the king!" he roared. "Easton, how could you?"

Easton's expression was cold and calculating. "I did what I had to do. The king was changing, becoming a threat. You were too blind to see it."

"So when I ordered you to protect the king, you let Lucien waltz right in?" Aiden demanded disbelief and fury etched on his face.

"Pretty much... It made my job a lot easier when you asked this of me instead of defending the castle and finding the opportune moment to sneak Lucien through."

When Easton finished his explanation, three guards entered the cottage, escorting Queen Sophie, Prince Cadeyrn, and Princess Amara. They were disheveled and frightened, the queen clutching her children close.

Lucien's eyes lit up with a sinister glee. "Oh, look who it is!" he cackled. "The royal family, what a treat!"

Aiden stepped forward, protective instincts kicking in. "Don't touch them!" he warned.

Lucien merely smirked. "And who's going to stop me?" he replied, gesturing to his followers.

Aiden hesitated. He could fight, but it would be futile against so many. He had to bide his time and wait for the right moment to strike. For now, he could only watch as the royal family was taken captive.

"Instead of killing us right away, Lucien threw us into the dungeons," Aiden recounted, his voice filled with a mixture of anger and despair. *"The queen, the prince, and the princess were crammed into a tiny cell, while the rest of us were thrown into filthy, overcrowded cells. We were given scraps of food once a week if we were lucky. The royal family was forced to serve as Lucien's slaves, working from dawn till dusk.*

"People who opposed Lucien's rule were hunted down and imprisoned. The dungeons became a place of suffering and death. Bodies piled up, left to rot. The stench was unbearable, the conditions inhumane. We endured months of torment, our spirits broken, our hope fading.

"As I watched the queen comfort her children, offering them her meager rations and singing them lullabies, a spark ignited within me. Her selfless love reminded me of the king's dying words: to protect the kingdom and its people. I knew I had to survive, to rise against Lucien's tyranny.

"It would be a long and perilous journey, but I was determined. I would bide my time, feign loyalty, and wait for the perfect moment to strike. Lucien, with his arrogance and cruelty, was a formidable foe. But I would not be defeated.

"Three months had passed, and the day of reckoning had arrived. Lucien's followers descended into the dungeon, chains in hand. The royal family and the remaining prisoners were dragged from their cells into the cold, unforgiving light of day."

A guillotine stood silent, a grim harbinger of death. The prisoners, including the royal family, were lined up, facing the ruins of their once-glorious city. The castle, now a crumbling shell, stood as a stark reminder of the destruction wrought by Lucien's tyranny. The vibrant, life-filled city had been reduced to a desolate wasteland, the magical glow of the trees extinguished.

"Now, my friends," Lucien declared, his voice echoing through the ruined city, "you have seen the power I wield. You have a choice: join me, or face the consequences." He paused, a sinister smile playing on his lips. "Just know... Those who refuse will pay the ultimate price."

The shackled prisoners stared at each other in bewilderment as the first person in line took his place in front of Lucien.

"Do you accept my offer to join my legion? We will be powerful yet."

"No." the man replied in a monotonous tone.

"Very well," Lucien responded rolling his eyes. "Guards!" He waved his hand, "You know what to do."

The audience watched as two of Lucien's guards escorted the man to the guillotine and watched in astonishment when the blade fell, chopping off the victim's head.

Lucien burst into laughter as everyone looked on in shock. "I told you if you reject my offer, you pay the ultimate price... you die!" He retorted jovially.

A gasp rippled through the crowd as Lucien's threat hung heavy in the air. "Bow down to your new king!" he roared.

One by one, the prisoners were forced to make a choice: submit or die. Most, fearing for their lives, chose to pledge allegiance to Lucien's twisted vision.

When it was Aiden's turn, he hesitated. A silent battle raged within him. Finally, with a heavy heart, he knelt before Lucien. "I join you, my king," he said, his voice barely a whisper.

Lucien broke out in hysterical laughter. "Splendid… Just splendid Aiden. I have many, many plans for you!" he smirked.

The royal family, spared from immediate death, were condemned to a life of servitude in the dungeons. Forced to witness the horrors inflicted upon their loyal subjects, they suffered both physically and emotionally. Aiden, burdened with guilt, watched helplessly as the once-vibrant kingdom fell into darkness. His duty to protect the royal family had failed, and he was now forced to serve a tyrant. The weight of his failure pressed heavily upon him.

Years had passed, and the kingdom had fallen into disarray. The once-vibrant city was now a shadow of its former self, with its people living in poverty and squalor. Lucien, the tyrant king, lived in opulence, surrounded by luxury and excess. He had everything he could desire: fine food, beautiful clothes, and a loyal following. The people, desperate and starving, resorted to bartering their most precious possessions for scraps of food. Crime ran rampant, as the king turned a blind eye to the suffering of his subjects.

Aiden, though a prisoner of the king, had managed to gain his trust. He was Lucien's confidant, his go-to for every decision. However, Easton remained skeptical, wary of Aiden's true intentions. Lucien, meanwhile, kept his plans shrouded in secrecy, sending his guards on mysterious missions to other realms. The nature of these missions remained a mystery, even to his most trusted confidant.

"I was jolted awake by Easton one night with his face etched in jealous anger. He informed me the King requested my presence immediately. I hurried out of bed and ran to his side of the castle. I found him standing, arms crossed behind his back, staring out the window as if he were in deep thought."

"You wished to see me, sir," Aiden announced his arrival along with Easton and Adam.

"Yes," the king replied, turning to face Aiden. "You've proven yourself to be a valuable asset. I've been watching you closely, and you've exceeded my expectations. But there's something you should know..." He paused, his expression turning serious. "When Aldrich died, he took his power with him. I'm not as powerful as I once was. That's why I've been sending you on those missions, gathering information and artifacts. We're so close to restoring my power, but there's still one piece missing."

"A girl," he said hesitantly, his voice filled with mystery and intrigue. "A girl from a realm we have never ventured into before."

Aiden's eyebrows raised in curiosity as he asked, "What is this girl supposed to be capable of?"

"She is meant to bring back my powers," the man replied, his tone grave and serious.

"But how, sir?" Aiden pressed for more information.

"She must perform a ritual, and then, if I so desire, she will become my wife," the man explained, his words dripping with anticipation.

Aiden's confusion grew as he questioned, "How is it possible for her to restore stolen powers? Only the royals have the authority to take away power, and it is believed that only they can return it. No one else is said to possess such a gift."

Lucien sighed, a look of frustration crossing his face. "I've been observing her for years. She's clumsy with her powers, unaware of their true potential. Yet, she has this uncanny ability to return to the same realm, Terrah, after each death. It's as if she's tied to that place, destined to live and die there. And her appearance... it never changes. She's a mystery, an enigma. A piece of the puzzle that doesn't quite fit."

He paused, lost in thought. "She's supposed to be part of Eternium, but she was never born here. It's a paradox, a cosmic anomaly."

"Why do you say she is supposed to be a part of Eternium?" Aiden asked curiously.

"Because her existence can threaten every being in Eternium. She possesses the abilities of the so-called royals but to such a point that they surpass their natural state.

"The kings before me knew of Ember," Lucien explained, his voice filled with a strange intensity. "But they never pursued her. Now, I have a greater purpose for her. She's a key to unlocking something far greater than we can imagine."

He paused, his eyes gleaming with a dark ambition. "Aiden… you, Easton, and Adam will travel to Terrah and find her. Bring her here, and give her this amulet. It will amplify her powers and make it easier for her to cross dimensions. She is the missing piece to our puzzle."

The three men bowed, their faces etched with determination. They walked to the old training courtyard that had not been used in years. Then, with a flash of blue light, they vanished.

"As we traveled between dimensions, I felt a strange pull, a magnetic force drawing me. I followed it to the land of Terrah, which led me straight to you. You were as beautiful back then as you are now. I saw you, I knew exactly where you were and from that point on, I knew I must protect you.

"Terrah is a huge land that would take Easton and Adam a long time to navigate for one girl. So I acted like I did not see you, shielding my mind from their prying eyes.

"When the day started to become night, we returned to Eternium to report our failure to find you to the king."

"YOU MUST FIND HER!!" Lucien demanded in desperation. "Go to your quarters… get out of my sight." He said disappointingly.

"The next day, we were sent back to Terrah, this time with reinforcements. Separating from the group, I began my search for you. It was during this time that I started training you, preparing you for the inevitable conflict. I knew I couldn't keep you hidden forever, but I tried my best to protect you.

"Easton, however, had been watching my every move. He knew what I was doing, but he chose to remain silent. A month later, he and his men ambushed us, capturing both you and me. As they dragged us back to Eternium, my heart ached with worry for your safety."

Imprisoned in the dark depths of the dungeon, Aiden endured days of relentless torture before being dragged before the king.

Ember stood by Lucien's side, her expression a canvas of fear.

"So, you thought you could conceal the girl from me, did you?" The king's voice was chillingly calm. "Easton, enlighten me on what you have discovered."

Easton stepped forward, a smirk dancing on his lips. "For weeks, Aiden has been straying from his duties, lingering in the realm of Terrah long past his allotted time. I found his behavior suspicious, so I took it upon myself to investigate. To my surprise, I discovered he had been fraternizing with the subject - Ember. I suspected he might be trying to lure her to Eternium, but instead, he was teaching her to harness her powers. It became clear he was defying your orders, my liege. And upon further investigation, I learned that Ember is not just any girl - she is Aiden's soulmate."

Aiden's gaze fell upon Ember, her eyes filled with fear. Lucien's eyes narrowed, a sinister smile creeping across his face. "What to do with you?" he mused. "Aiden, you were a loyal soldier, but your betrayal cannot go unpunished. I banish you from Eternium."

"But this is my home!" Aiden protested.

"A shame," Lucien replied, his tone cold. "But if you ever return, you will face the ultimate consequence."

"What about Ember?" Aiden asked his concern for her was evident.

"Don't worry about her," Lucien said, a cruel smile spreading across his face. "She'll be *just* fine."

Before Aiden could say something else, he disappeared.

Aiden let go of me, the memories were over. "All I can recall from that fateful day is the haunting smirk etched on his face as I was condemned to Terrah for eternity."

"What happened to me?" I asked, my voice heavy with sadness.

"I don't know for sure. I was busy going through different options to get back to you when two days later you died..." he replied, his voice filled with regret. "I felt you die..."

"How?" I asked, confused.

"It's a part of our abilities when we meet our soulmates… Whenever your soulmate dies, there is an unexplainable feeling of loss that can never go away."

"I died?" I echoed, stunned.

"Yes, my love. I'm not sure if Lucien killed you, or if you killed yourself, or maybe the ritual he spoke of was too powerful for you."

I was silent for a long moment, trying to process this new information. "Is there any way to access those memories?" I asked, hopeful.

"I don't think so," he replied. "We've tried before, but it hasn't worked."

"Then how did I access those memories when I was in that house in the forest?" I questioned.

"I honestly don't know," he admitted, his voice filled with uncertainty.

Chapter Eleven
Training Days

Two months had passed since Aiden had shown me the wonders of Eternium. Under his tutelage, I'd rapidly grown stronger, our training sessions often taking place in a secluded woodland. Calix, Aiden's enigmatic friend, joined us. He was a being from beyond time and space, a cosmic wanderer with a vast knowledge of the universe. Unlike Aiden and I, who were bound to specific realms, Calix was unbound, a timeless entity.

However, even Calix had limits. His mind, though vast, couldn't contain the entirety of the universe's knowledge. To delve too deep into his ancestral memory risked overloading his mind. As for me, being a latecomer to this cosmic drama, I lacked the innate connection to the universe that Aiden and Calix possessed. My memories were fragmented, lost to the mists of time.

Calix possesses physical characteristics reminiscent of Aiden, standing at an impressive 6'2" with a medium build that tends towards slimness. Despite his seemingly small and sinewy muscles, they are actually three times more abundant than average and eight to ten times denser, along with his bones. Aiden had begun to open up about his unique physique, which set him apart from others, yet both Aiden and Calix appeared perfectly proportioned.

Under Calix's tutelage, I have been immersed in rigorous training from dawn to dusk, honing my skills in hand-to-hand combat, swordsmanship, and archery. Both of them were a little disappointed in me the first few weeks because I had never had to wield a sword before. It's the 21st century, give me a break! However, where there was disappointment, there was also astonishment, even on my part, at my natural aptitude for archery. With just a few adjustments to my stance, I was well on my way to mastering the bow and arrow.

It was during one of these "adjustments" that I learned of Calix's bisexuality, with a slight preference towards men. I couldn't help but feel a slight pressure on my back as he stood closely behind me, as I felt pressure on my back while he was closely pressed up against me with his groin.

"Hey!" I exclaimed, my tone accusatory. As I glanced at him, I noticed his gaze fixed on Aiden's glistening, sweaty body as he worked out, drool practically escaping his mouth.

"Huh?" Calix responded, clearly confused by my outburst until he finally understood the source of my irritation. "Oh, honey, this isn't meant for you!"

"I've noticed…" I replied with a half-smile, joining his gaze in appreciating Aiden's physique.

Although Aiden demonstrated exceptional skill as a combat instructor, as evidenced by the vivid memories he shared with me from his time at Eternium, he believed it would be more advantageous for everyone if he focused on teaching me how to shield myself from telepathic intrusion. Calix, unable to instruct me in this particular skill, decided to divide their responsibilities accordingly. Aiden proved to be an excellent teacher, drawing on his experience training soldiers to guide me in this new endeavor. However, his ingrained military mindset occasionally resurfaces, causing him to be more demanding and rigorous in his approach than usual.

The mental disciplines proved to be the most challenging aspect of my training. Blocking out others' thoughts was one thing, but actively shielding my own was a whole different beast. It was like trying to build an invisible fortress around my mind, a constant and exhausting effort.

As I struggled with the mental exercises, Calix watched from a distance, a serene expression on his face. Aiden, my patient instructor, offered guidance. "Imagine a barrier, a wall between your thoughts and the outside world," he instructed. "The stronger the barrier, the harder it is for others to intrude."

It was a complex task, akin to deflecting a sword without revealing one's guard. I had to both defend my thoughts and conceal my intentions, a delicate balance that required constant vigilance.

My thoughts began to drift, shifting focus to other topics such as Sara, or the potential consequences if Lucien were to find me, and what he might do. As my mind raced, Aiden intervened.

"Ember, calm down. You'll get the hang of it soon," he reassured me.

"But not soon enough Aiden!" I yelled aggravated. "My birthday is almost here and I'm just as screwed as I was two months ago!" My frustration turned to self-directed anger, then despair. "What if I can't do this?"

Aiden's expression softened, and he flashed the smile that always warmed my heart. "You will, Ember," he said, kissing me and gently squeezing my hand. "You are stronger than you realize, my love."

"We have visitors!" Calix exclaimed, leaping to his feet and dashing towards us. The three of us stood together, anticipating the appearance of the intruders. "One of them is Easton," Aiden remarked with a hint of disdain. Emerging from the shadows were two figures: Sara and Easton.

Calix swiftly prepared his weapon, while Aiden positioned himself protectively in front of me. "What are you doing here, Easton?" Aiden demanded.

"I'm not here to cause harm or betray anyone," Easton replied, his gaze fixed on me. "I've come to offer my assistance."

"Help?" Calix chuckled. "Just like how you assisted Aiden by stealing his girl away from him multiple times? Or when you betrayed him to protect King Aldrich? Or the time you orchestrated his banishment? Or perhaps when you ended his life?"

Sara gazed down at her feet, her expression filled with disappointment.

"I understand that you all have doubts about me, but once I prove myself, I am confident you will trust me. I was initially sent here to monitor Ember, but then I met Sara... She is my soulmate. He knows Sara is Ember's best friend and he is planning on using her as leverage. Lucien knows she wouldn't let her friend die because of her and I can't allow him to take her from me." Easton pleaded to the group. "Please, Ember...." He began as he started to take a step towards the group.

Calix quickly moved toward Easton, placing the point of the blade at his throat, "Take one more step and it will be your last... I dare you to give me a reason." He threatened with a cold tone.

Aiden scrutinized him from head to toe before asking, "What makes you think we will help you?"

"For one, Ember will never forgive you if anything happened to Sara."

Anger came over me as I shouted, "It's your fault we are in this mess in the first place asshole!"

Everyone became quiet for a few minutes as they waited for something miraculous to happen. When it didn't, the guest continued to argue. As they were busy and completely oblivious to their surroundings at this moment, I walked over to Sara and hugged her. We hadn't talked in a while and the poor thing looked to be in shock.

"Are you okay?" I asked, gently pulling her away from Easton.

"I just... I didn't know," she stammered, tears welling up in her eyes. "I'm so sorry, Ember."

"For what?" I asked, confused.

"For everything," she replied, her voice breaking. "I didn't know... I want to hate him, but I can't."

"Don't worry about it, Sara," I said, trying to comfort her. "There's nothing to apologize for."

"I should have listened to you from the start," Sara admitted, her voice filled with regret.

"Listen, there's nothing to worry about. I understand how much you want to hate him, but this connection won't allow you to."

With that, we turned back to the group, ready to face whatever was happening between Aiden and Easton.

Calix maintained the sharp edge of his blade against Easton's neck. "Should you attempt any harm towards Aiden or Ember, rest assured I will not hesitate to take you down," he declared, his expression devoid of emotion.

"Ok guys, put your dicks away!" I yelled as I walked up to them holding Sara's hand.

The three men appeared visibly agitated. Calix calmly sheathed his weapon, breaking the tense silence that hung in the air as they locked eyes with each other.

"How did you find us?" I asked Sara.

"It wasn't hard," Easton replied, his eyes still fixed on Aiden and Calix, trying to get another rise out of them.

"Actually, Ember told me where you were…" Sara admitted.

I stared at her confused. "No, I didn't."

Sara looked at me, guilty.

Aiden turned his head disapprovingly toward me. "Well, now we can't go back to your house. We need to find a new place to stay."

"Why?" I asked, confused.

"If Lucien is truly seeking to capture Sara to reach you, then both of you are at risk." He gives a disgusted side-eye to Easton, "If he doesn't turn Sara over himself."

Easton bristled at the accusation. "I would never."

"Lucien will send others to come find both of you. We just better hope he hasn't already sent out some spies."

"But what about my brother's wedding?" I protested.

"We can't risk it," Calix said. "Your safety is more important."

I stood there, feeling a mix of disappointment and fear. I'd never been camping before, and the thought of living in the wilderness terrified me. And to top it all off, I couldn't trust anyone, not even Sara. What had my life become?

Chapter Twelve
The Faceless Man

I told my parents and brother that I'd be spending a few weeks with Sara, visiting a relative of hers. I assured them I'd be back in time for Will's wedding, whenever that might be. After saying my quick goodbyes to my family, Sara, Easton, Calix, Aiden, and I set off on our journey south. We eventually found a secluded spot in the Georgia wilderness, a perfect hidden haven.

As we sat around the campfire, a tense silence hung in the air. The only sounds were the crackling fire and the distant chirping of crickets. Determined to break the ice, I started a conversation.

"So, Easton," I began, "since we're being honest, where were you in January when we were investigating that abandoned building? You know, the one where you came back with that strange locket?"

"Well..." Easton began, taken aback by my sudden question. "I guess you already figured out that after high school, I went back to Eternium. I already reported every detail I needed about you to Lucien. He didn't think there was any reason for me to stay until you were twenty-one. I mean, you never went out to do anything so there wasn't any risk in leaving you to your own devices.

"Lucien kept tabs on you, entering your dreams. It shouldn't come as a surprise that I happened to 'bump' into you the same day you had a dream about Aiden. I was sent to keep an eye on you and report back if Aiden ever made contact.

"So, the reason you were originally attracted to that building was because Aiden was somewhere around there. While you were on the phone, I went inside to find him, but he was no longer there. That's when I decided to jump back to Eternium to let Lucien know that Aiden was near. That's when he ordered me to hurry with the plan. But when I came back, I found you on the sidewalk freaking out. I had to calm you down before handing you the locket because it would have reacted to your emotions."

"How could it do that?" I asked incredulously. " And why is my age so important?"

"When you turn twenty-one, your powers blossom, a secret garden of extraordinary abilities. While you may not wield them consciously, they're at their most potent. The locket, a guardian, taps into this potential, regardless of your age. It offers a guiding hand, a way to harness your powers. The amulet, however, is a fickle ally. Used wisely, it's a force multiplier. But misused, it can turn against you, feeding on your emotions and wreaking havoc."

"Is it like magic or something? Can Ember only use it?" Sara asked.

"It's not exactly magic… Other people could use it, but it wouldn't be as effective because it was only meant for Ember." Aiden cut in.

"It was my responsibility to persuade you to wear the locket, Ember," Easton explained, his tone serious. "But your intense emotions could have had catastrophic consequences, potentially destroying the entire universe."

"Why do I need to wear it?" I asked, feeling anxious about the possibility of causing reality to collapse.

"The locket is set to bring you to Eternium. With it, you could technically travel to different dimensions, as you are not originally from our realm and lack the innate ability to do so," Easton clarified. "It is also the key to unlock more of your power. However, by enhancing your abilities, Lucien believes you can return his powers and even strengthen Eternium."

I was speechless, unable to process the information. Shock and fear gripped me, rendering me unable to respond.

"Why this sudden change of heart?" Aiden spat, disgust lacing his tone. "It can't be just because you found your precious soulmate, and Lucien, in his twisted way, has threatened her as bait. He wouldn't harm her. He'd just pretend to, to get to Ember."

Easton remained silent, his jaw clenched. A heavy sigh escaped his lips before he muttered, "I'm doing this for Sara. She didn't ask. I didn't have to explain anything to her, but I did..."

"So, finding your 'true love' makes you a hero now? I don't buy it. And what about all the other soulmates you've murdered? The ones you deemed 'impossible' or 'liabilities'? Is this how you repay their sacrifices?" Calix roared, fury burning in his eyes.

Guilt and shame warred on Easton's face. Sara, wide-eyed, looked horrified. Aiden and Calix held Easton's gaze, their silent judgment cutting deeper than any words.

"I didn't *understand*..." Easton's voice was a mere whisper, a stark contrast to his usual confident tone. "I'm not here to hurt Ember. I'm here to help, for Sara. Despite my past mistakes, I *truly* understand the wrong I've done... especially to you, Aiden."

Calix's gaze bore into Easton, his voice laced with bitter irony. "There's one thing you *still* don't understand: love can transform a person. It can make them brave, make them better."

A heavy silence settled over them, each word hanging in the air, a stark reminder of the past and the uncertain future.

"You think you can make amends, Easton? You burned that bridge long ago. Don't be surprised if it can't be rebuilt." Aiden's words hung in the air as he stormed away, leaving a trail of icy silence.

Calix, his voice a low growl, turned back to Easton. "You may smooth-talk your way out of anything and hell, you could probably run for president in this world with your lies but don't think you've fooled me. If you dare harm Aiden, Ember, or Sara, or if I discover your true intentions, you'll wish you'd never been born." He turned to me, his tone softening. "Come on, Ember. You need rest, and Aiden wouldn't want you alone with this... traitor."

As I stood up to walk away with Calix, Easton started talking again, "Ember, I can help you hone your skills. Other than Lucien, I am probably the only other person who has seen all of them."

"I'm not so sure about that..." I trailed off, doubt etched across my face.

"With your birthday just around the corner, wouldn't you want to harness your full potential?" he pressed, his voice laced with a dangerous promise.

"How do I know you're not playing me?" I countered, my eyes narrowing.

"Ember, please," Sara pleaded, her voice filled with desperation. "Give him a chance."

"I'm sorry, Sara, but you haven't seen what I've seen. You don't know what this man is capable of." I retorted, my tone firm.

"In return, I'll reveal Lucien's secrets. I'll tell you where his followers hide, their plans, and how to stay off their radar," Easton offered, his voice smooth as silk.

I regarded him with skepticism. "And how do you know Lucien hasn't already turned the tables on you?"

"He's trapped in his realm, forced to rely on his followers' reports. He might still have his telepathy, but he can't breach my mind. I've made sure of it. He'll believe whatever I tell him."

A shiver ran down my spine, not from fear, but from a strange unease. There was nothing overtly threatening in his words, yet a deep-seated unease gnawed at me.

Calix, sensing my discomfort, pulled me away from Easton. "Are you alright?" he asked, concern etched on his face.

"I don't know..." I murmured, lost in thought.

"Do you trust him?" he pressed.

"There's something... off about his last statement," I admitted.

"Don't overthink it for now," he soothed. "We'll figure out his true intentions soon enough... hopefully."

"Hopefully," I echoed, lost in thought. Then, a question popped into my head. "Have you ever... had a soulmate?"

Calix chuckled. "Why do you ask?"

"It's just... you seemed so passionate about Easton's past mistakes, especially the part about killing soulmates."

"No, honey," he replied, a playful smile on his lips. "I've just enjoyed the thrill of the moment. I'm not one for forever. I like to have fun."

"Then why did you get so upset?" I pressed.

"Because I care about you and Aiden. He's like a brother, and you're like a sister. He's deeply in love with you, and I understand the whole soulmate thing. But he never gets the time he deserves to spend with you."

"Where is he now?" I questioned.

"Probably cooling off," Calix replied, his tone casual.

"Someone who's betrayed him numerous times shows up, and he leaves me, the person he claims to protect?" I scoffed.

"It's not that simple, Ember. He just needs to calm down. Besides, I'm here with you. And Aiden knows I'd never let anything happen to you," he reassured me with a comforting smile as we reached the tents. "Now, get some rest. I'll keep watch." He kissed my forehead gently. "Sleep tight."

****

As soon as I fell asleep, I was plunged into a familiar nightmare. The desolate city, the dim, eerie glow of streetlamps, and the looming shadow of Lucien. But this time, fear would not be my master. I would not cower. I would not run.

Lucien watched, a sinister smile playing on his lips. The shadows danced at his command, but I remained unmoved. My defiance seemed to anger him, the ground trembling beneath my feet. Yet, I stood firm, my resolve unwavering.

I approached the shattered remains of a car, a grotesque figure moaning within. With a deep breath, I moved closer, the ground shaking violently as the entity turned to face me.

My resolve wavered as I stumbled backward. A cacophony of maniacal laughter echoed through the desolate landscape, jolting me back to reality. I took a deep breath, steeling myself against the fear. The faceless creature lunged forward, a hideous screech tearing through the silence. I stood firm, refusing to yield.

A strange sense of familiarity washed over me. There was something more to this creature, something beyond its monstrous exterior. But how could I unlock its secrets?

Without conscious thought, I reached out and grasped its shoulder. In an instant, the world shifted. I was no longer in the desolate city. Darkness enveloped me, a void devoid of light or sound. I fumbled blindly, searching for a wall, a door, or anything to guide me. Surely, I would eventually stumble upon something. But then, a swift movement caught my eye.

Something, or someone, darted past me, disappearing into the darkness.

A deafening boom jolted me, a blinding light engulfing my vision. When my eyes finally adjusted, I found myself trapped in a cold, metallic cell. A figure huddled in the corner, whimpering softly. Even from a distance, I could see it wasn't the disfigured creature. This was a boy, clad in tattered, filthy clothes.

"Hello?" I called out, hoping for an explanation.

The boy flinched at the sound of my voice. "Who... who are you? What are you doing here?" he stammered, his voice trembling.

"My name's Ember, and to be honest, I have no idea. I don't know how I got here, or how to get out." But I had a hunch this boy was the key to my escape.

"You shouldn't be here. You'll anger him..."

"Who?" I pressed.

The child didn't answer, his fear palpable. He stood, hunched over, avoiding my gaze.

"It's okay, sweetie," I soothed. "You don't have to tell me if you don't want to. So, how did you get here?"

"He locked me in here a long time ago. I don't even remember how long."

Pity washed over me. He was clearly terrified. I could see the fear in his eyes, his trembling hands. I decided to change the subject, to ease the tension and gain his trust. "What's your name?" I asked gently.

"Lucien."

My heart sank. A wave of nausea washed over me. "How... how is that possible?" I stammered, backing away. "You're joking, right?"

"No."

I paced the small cell, my mind racing. "How is that possible? I've seen him through others' memories, and you look nothing like him."

"I'm the Lucien before the fall," he explained with a hint of sadness in his voice. "Before the King stripped me of my powers. Before the darkness consumed me. I'm the Lucien before the corruption."

"Why?" I pressed, seeking answers.

He hesitated as a flicker of pain crossed his eyes. "Whenever he locked me away, he transformed me into that monster. When the King took my powers, I was trapped within that hideous form."

"What is that thing?" I asked, fear creeping into my voice.

"It's Lucien. It's how he sees himself, how he feels. The King, in his arrogance, sought to destroy the vain, prideful creature I once was."

"But the King was supposed to be kind, just," I protested.

"He was. And he still could be."

"How old were you when you were locked away?" I inquired.

Lucien paused, lost in thought. "I was about sixteen."

My jaw dropped. "You were so young... What happened? What caused you to become... corrupted?"

Before he could finish, the room began to shake violently.

"NO MORE!" a booming voice echoed, filling the air.

I blinked, disoriented. I was back on the cracked pavement, the familiar city skyline looming overhead. I looked up at the window, recognizing where I was: the scene of Sara's tragic death.

A surge of adrenaline coursed through me as I raced around the building, searching for an entrance.

"You cannot enter!" Lucien's voice boomed, a sinister undertone.

The room transformed before my eyes. The dust and cobwebs vanished, replaced by pristine furniture and freshly painted walls adorned with elegant portraits.

The door burst open, and Sara was shoved inside, her body hitting the floor with a sickening thud. As she scrambled to her feet, I watched, my heart pounding. Instead of panicking, I forced myself to remain calm, to observe every detail. The door swung open again, and Sara was on her knees, begging for mercy. Then, a blinding flash of light consumed the scene, obscuring the final moments of her life.

The room returned to its dilapidated state, the horrifying vision fading. *What was happening? What is all of this?*

Lucien materialized before me, his eyes glowing with malice. My heart pounded, but I refused to show fear. "You've been a naughty girl, Ember," he sneered.

"How so?" I retorted, my voice filled with disgust.

"First, you interacted with my benevolent, gullible, and weak fifteen-year-old self. A pity, really. I should have hidden him better. But destroying him was ultimately the better choice. Why keep him around? Foolish of me."

"You..."

"I'm not finished!" Lucien roared, his voice a thunderclap. "You also refused to act to save your friend. Tsk, tsk. Disappointing, Ember. How do you think she'd feel knowing her best friend did nothing but watch her die?"

"I'm sure that whatever Sara you conjured up is better off dead. Seems like you did her a favor," I retorted, my voice hard. I knew that the Sara in the vision wasn't the real one, protected by Easton. I was trying to convince him that killing her was a twisted form of mercy. Torturing her would be more his style, but killing her would spare her further suffering.

The cloaked figure, a manifestation of Lucien's darker self, loomed over me. His face, inches from mine, was a mask of malevolent intent. As he studied me, I stood defiant, refusing to flinch or flee. My body yearned to run, but my mind held firm.

"And why did you keep your younger self locked away?" I challenged. "You're hardly sentimental. Why hide him, why destroy him?"

"He was weak," Lucien sneered. "A child, believing in a world of sugar and spice. He had to be hidden, destroyed. It was the only way."

"You said you destroyed him," I countered.

"He's merely... dormant," Lucien replied, a sinister smile playing on his lips. "You won't be meddling any longer."

"That's a shame," I retorted. "I rather liked him."

"Oh, look at you, all attitude," Lucien chuckled. "I like that."

I felt a wave of nausea rise in my stomach as he leaned in closer. "Back off," I warned, my voice steady.

"Or else what?" he taunted. "You're trapped here until I say so."

"We'll see about that," I retorted, my defiance unwavering.

Chapter Thirteen
New Instruction

As the morning light filtered through the trees, I awoke from the clutches of my nightmare, feeling a surge of triumph like never before. A smile crept across my face, a rare occurrence after battling my nightmares for so long.

Yawning and stretching, I readied myself for the day ahead. The sun was just beginning to rise, casting a warm glow over the camp. The chill in the air hinted at the lingering winter, but the promise of spring was in the air, bringing with it the hope of warmer days ahead.

Peering out of my tent, I caught sight of Calix, peacefully asleep with his sword by his side. He must have stayed up late, keeping watch to ensure my safety. I wondered if Aiden had returned from his walk, and how long Calix had been guarding me.

Rubbing the sleep from my eyes, I thought I saw a figure standing in the distance. Straining my eyes to focus, I found nothing there. Yet, a sense of unease lingered, casting a shadow over the peaceful morning.

I was too exhausted to give the matter more thought, so I rose and began to pace around. I reached out and shook Calix's shoulder, calling out his name.

"Calix, wake up!" I exclaimed.

He sprang to his feet, looking bewildered. "What happened? What's going on?" he asked.

I couldn't help but laugh at his reaction. "Relax, commando, nothing is happening."

He let out a long yawn. "Why are you up so early?"

"Just accustomed to our early training sessions, I suppose," I explained.

"I believe you deserve a day off," he suggested as he headed back to his tent.

"Oh... Alright," I responded, feeling a little disappointed. "By the way, did you happen to see if Aiden returned?"

Calix was already settled in his tent, his voice barely audible as he said, "I haven't seen him," followed by a chorus of snores.

What should I do now? Aiden would be furious if I ventured off in search of him, especially with all the dangers lurking out here, particularly Easton and some of Lucien's followers. With Calix asleep, I found myself with nothing to occupy my time and no one to keep me company. *How long does it take for a guy to cool off?* I wondered as I settled onto a tree stump, absentmindedly playing with a stick in the dirt. Lost in my thoughts, time slipped away until my stomach growled with hunger, snapping me back to reality.

There was no use in waking Sleeping Beauty, so perhaps I should seek out Aiden or Sara instead. What if Easton and Sara had already left after the boys' spat last night? Regardless, the prospect of searching for someone, even if it meant encountering my abductor, seemed more appealing than the current boredom I was experiencing.

I left a note for Calix to reassure him that I had not been abducted while he was asleep. I wanted to ensure he knew I was safe, but the reality was that anything could happen once I left camp - from falling into a hole to encountering a bear or wolf.

As I ventured through the forest, the uneasiness I had felt earlier lingered. I couldn't shake the feeling that someone, or something, was following me. Every time I turned around, there was no one in sight. I tried to convince myself it was just a deer or rabbit, but the fear of encountering a dangerous animal like a bear crept into my mind.

My imagination ran wild, conjuring up terrifying scenarios that made me increasingly anxious. The eerie silence of the forest only added to my growing sense of dread.

A mysterious figure darted swiftly between the trees, its silhouette resembling that of a human, yet moving with an unnatural speed. My heart raced as I quickened my pace, desperately hoping to either stumble upon Aiden or locate Sara and Easton without delay.

As I began to jog, my footsteps echoed loudly on the forest floor, each one accompanied by a resounding crunch and thud. Suddenly, I froze in my tracks, convinced I had heard a faint whisper calling my name. I turned around, squinting into the darkness in search of a familiar face, but found nothing.

Taking a deep breath, I tried to calm my racing heart, convincing myself that it was all in my head. Just as I turned to continue on my way, a wave of terror washed over me. My chest tightened, my mouth went dry, my palms grew clammy, and my body trembled with fear as I struggled to draw a breath. To my horror, the cloaked shadow figure loomed ominously above me.

"Lucien?" I whispered, disbelief etched on my face.

He chuckled, a chilling sound that sent shivers down my spine. "Yes, it's me, Ember."

"But... how?" I stammered. "You're powerless."

He sneered, his eyes filled with malice. "Powerless? I have all the power I need to find you, to torment you, to make your life a living nightmare until you join me."

A surge of anger coursed through me. I remembered Easton's warning about Lucien's plans for Sara. "You can't be here," I growled. "You're not real."

He laughed, a sound that seemed to echo through the void. "Oh, but I am, Ember. As real as you are."

"You need to leave! Go back to your own realm!" I cried, desperation fueling my voice.

A familiar voice cut through the air. "Ember?" Aiden's confused gaze met mine. "What are you doing?"

I turned back to where Lucien had stood, but he was gone.

"Are you alright?" Aiden asked concern growing on his face.

"No... Lucien..." Tears welled up in my eyes. "He was here."

Aiden's expression turned grave. "That's not possible..." he muttered, his eyes scanning my face.

"Where were you?" I asked through sobs.

He pulled me into a comforting embrace, stroking my hair. His voice was gentle as he explained, "Last night, Easton's words haunted me. I was afraid of his intentions, so I left to keep an eye on him. I watched him, waited for him to make a move, to try to drag you to Eternium. But he never did. I think he's biding his time, waiting for the perfect moment to strike."

"How did you find me?" I asked, my voice filled with wonder.

He gazed into my eyes, a tender smile playing on his lips. "Ember, you should know by now. No matter where you are, I'll always find you." He leaned in and kissed me softly. "Where's Calix?"

My voice steadied as I replied, "He's asleep in his tent. I think he stayed up all night, keeping watch."

Aiden's smile widened, relieved to know his friend was looking after me. "Why wasn't he with you?" he asked, a hint of concern in his voice.

"I... I went looking for you," I confessed, my voice trailing off.

He gave me a stern look, the kind a parent gives a misbehaving child. "You know you shouldn't wander off alone," he scolded gently.

I hung my head, shame washing over me. "I know... I'm sorry. I just wanted to find you."

Aiden softened his expression. "It's okay. Nothing happened, so no harm done."

A sudden pang of worry struck me. "Have you seen Sara?" I asked.

Aiden's face grew serious. "Yeah, she's fine. She and Easton stayed by the fire most of the night."

"Can we go see her?" I pleaded.

Aiden hesitated. "I suppose so. But please, keep your distance from Easton."

Relief washed over me. As we walked, I recounted my nightmare and my escape from Lucien's clutches. Aiden was both proud and astonished. He'd never seen me break free of Lucien's hold before, and he was shocked to learn about the younger version of Lucien.
"Well, it's true that you can't kill your former self," Aiden mused. "Your past is always with you, no matter how hard you try to bury it. I'm sure you'll confront it again, sooner or later."

I recounted my encounter with Lucien, describing how he'd appeared before I'd even reached Aiden. Aiden was stunned. This was a new twist, something they hadn't experienced in their past lives.

A long silence followed as Aiden pondered the possibilities. "He can't physically leave his realm," he finally said. "And he can't travel with one of his followers, not after the King stripped him of his power. There's only one other explanation: he must have used his telepathic abilities in a way we've never seen before."

I tilted my head, confusion etched on my face. "I don't understand."

"He found a way to link himself to you years ago, through your dreams," Aiden explained, his voice somber. "He could create terrifying worlds, torment you, and even inflict physical pain. He gained access to your memories, allowing him to manipulate your fears."

"But I saw him," I insisted, my voice trembling.

Aiden shook his head, lost in thought. "No, I didn't. I felt your presence, a strange pull, and caught a glimpse of you out of the corner of my eye. But he can't be here physically. It just doesn't add up."

Tears welled up in my eyes, threatening to spill over. The realization of Lucien's power, his ability to invade my dreams and now, my waking reality, was terrifying.

"My love, what's wrong?" Aiden's voice, gentle yet firm, interrupted my spiraling thoughts. The more he focused on me, the harder it became to regain my composure. "Baby, I believe you," he reassured me, his eyes filled with empathy. Then, his gaze turned inward, delving into the depths of my mind. "Hey," he said softly, tilting my chin upward, "I didn't say it was impossible, just improbable."

My heart ached. "That doesn't make me feel better," I admitted, my voice barely a whisper.

Aiden let out a long, weary sigh, not one of frustration, but of deep concern. "Well, we're going to see Sara anyway. Let's see if Easton has any answers," he suggested, his voice laced with determination.

I nodded, taking a deep breath to steady myself.

"Okay," he soothed, taking my hand in his. Aiden kissed my forehead, his touch gentle and comforting. "We'll figure this out. Just remember, I'm always here to protect you. Lucien, on the other hand, will try to deceive you, to break you, to shatter your mind. He isolates his victims, making them feel alone and vulnerable. It's easy to prey on the lonely."

I nodded, my heart heavy with understanding. "I know."

****

The path seemed to stretch on endlessly, a stark contrast to the memories of our journey here. Lost in thought, I barely noticed the passage of time. Aiden, ever the silent guardian, respected my solitude. Perhaps he feared breaking the fragile peace I'd found. Or maybe he simply didn't know what to say. Whatever the reason, I was grateful for the quiet companionship.

As we finally reached the fire, Sara leaped to her feet, a wide smile illuminating her face. "Oh, Ember! I thought I'd never see you again!" she exclaimed, rushing forward for a hug.

"Why would you think that?" I asked, pulling away from Sara's embrace.

"Easton told me how important you are," she explained, her voice filled with concern. "I was afraid I'd never see you again."

"Don't worry," I reassured her, glancing at Aiden, who stood silently behind me. "Nothing's going to happen to me. I actually came to check on you. But something strange happened on the way here, and I need to talk to Easton. Maybe he can shed some light on it." I scanned the area, noticing Sara was alone. "Where is he?"

"He went to Eternium about an hour ago," she replied. "Lucien needs the latest information, so Easton had to go."

"Wait a minute," Aiden interrupted, his voice laced with anger. "He left you here alone? After last night's scare?"

"He didn't have a choice," Sara defended. "Besides, I made him go. There's no one out here to hurt me."

"Okay, everyone, let's calm down," I interjected, stepping between the two. "Why didn't you come to find Aiden or me?"

"Because last night was a disaster. He was just trying to confess," Sara explained, her voice laced with frustration.

Aiden remained silent, his anger palpable.

"Sara, you have to understand," I said gently. "Easton and Aiden have a long history, a deep-seated rivalry that is older than us. A sudden change of heart isn't enough to erase the past. They may be working together now, but their animosity runs deep. Don't expect them to be best friends anytime soon."

Sara nodded, her anger dissipating. "You're right," she admitted. "He should be back soon. And Aiden, you're welcome to stay, though we both know you would anyway."

Aiden raised an eyebrow. "Why do you have a problem with me, Sara?"

"I don't," she replied, her tone flat. "I just... I feel protective of Easton. You two have a history of hurt. I don't want Ember and my friendship to be a casualty of your feud." She sighed. "We could end up like those siblings who can't stand each other because of their spouses."

"They choose to be uncivilized," Aiden retorted, "while we're bound by fate. Trust me, I'd never stand in the way of Ember's happiness, or yours."

As we waited for Easton, a tense silence hung in the air. I'd forgotten about hunger, so consumed by the strange events unfolding around me.

A blinding flash of light erupted from the trees, followed by a deafening crack. Aiden sprang to his feet, his body tense, ready for battle. Easton emerged from the tree line, his expression as cold as the winter wind. He paused, his eyes darting with a flicker of emotion before returning to their usual icy state.

Sara ran towards him, a kiss on his cheek a warm contrast to the chilling atmosphere.

"I told you I'd be fine!" Sara exclaimed, her voice filled with excitement.

Easton returned a forced smile. "Why are they here?" he asked, his voice laced with suspicion.

"Ask them yourself," Sara replied, a playful glint in her eyes.

Aiden's gaze swept across the forest, his body tense, ready for any threat.

"It's just me, Aiden," Easton began, releasing Sara from his grip. "I told Lucien I didn't know where you or Ember were. I haven't seen either of you in days."

Aiden's skepticism was palpable. The tension between the two men was thick, an unspoken battle brewing. Aiden's jaw clenched, his knuckles white, while Easton maintained a facade of calm.

"Oh, come on, you two!" I exclaimed, frustration boiling over. "Easton, we need to know why I just saw Lucien in the woods!"

He stared at me, his eyes wide with disbelief. "You... you saw him?"

"Yes, I did," I replied, growing impatient. "Do you know what's going on or not?"

"I do... but I didn't think he was capable of this."

"Capable of what?" I demanded.

"Telepathy is more than just communication," he explained, his voice heavy with worry. "He's always manipulated your dreams, kept you trapped. But you broke free, and that has angered him. He's growing stronger, and he's aware of Aiden's training. Whatever you did in that dream, it rattled him to the core."

I opened my mouth to speak, but he cut me off. "And I don't want to know the details. The less I know, the safer you and Sara are. But we're all in danger. Lucien is astral projecting."

"What's that?" I asked, my curiosity piqued. I knew the concept, but the implications were terrifying.

Aiden's body tensed. His face was a mask of concern. "Astral projection," he explained, his voice barely a whisper. "It's an out-of-body experience, a way to travel outside of one's physical form. While awake, asleep, or in deep meditation, one's consciousness can leave their body and explore other realms."

"Can anyone see someone who's projecting?" I asked, intrigued by the idea.

"No," Easton replied, his voice heavy. "It depends on whether the projector wants to be seen, or if the other person is sensitive. And that's what makes our situation so dangerous, Ember."

"Why?" I pressed, a sense of dread creeping over me.

"Because if he appeared to you in that form, he knows where you are," Easton explained, his voice low. "He could be watching us right now, and we wouldn't even know it."

A heavy silence fell over the group as the gravity of his words settled.

"Aiden, we need to teach her how to close her mind," Easton suggested. "It's too easy for Lucien and his followers to find her. We should move to a new location."

Aiden nodded, his expression grim.

"I'd be happy to teach her," Easton offered with a hint of challenge in his voice.

"Not a chance," Aiden retorted, his tone icy.

I turned to Aiden, desperation in my eyes. "Maybe we should let him help. You or Calix could supervise and make sure he doesn't do anything. It's worth a shot. We're all in danger if I don't..."

Aiden hesitated, his gaze unwavering. "If you try anything, anything at all, you'll regret it," he warned Easton.

Chapter Fourteen
Mind Fortress

The dingy motel room was a mere pit stop on our journey, a brief respite before we plunged back into the wilderness. Now, as we sat in the heart of this new forest, tension crackled in the air. Sara, Aiden, and Calix kept a watchful eye on us, their presence a constant reminder of the danger that lurked in the shadows.

Easton and I had spent the past hour practicing basic telepathic techniques. A simple warm-up, he'd called it, a precursor to the more complex lessons that would determine our fate. The others watched intently, their curiosity a double-edged sword. It provided a distraction, but it also made me self-conscious.

"You've done well so far with blocking thoughts," Easton said, his voice low. "But what I'm about to teach you won't be easy."

"Nothing has been easy so far," I replied, my tone weary.

"Yeah, well, what I'm about to show you will make everything else seem like a walk in the park," Easton warned, a glint of challenge in his eyes.

Dread washed over me. I'd struggled for weeks to master these abilities. Compared to Aiden and Easton, I was a novice, a mere child playing with powers far beyond my comprehension. Doom loomed large.

"This will require intense focus and concentration," Easton continued. "Aiden has taught you to block thoughts, right?"

"A little," I admitted, my voice barely a whisper.

Easton's impatience was palpable, though he maintained his composure. "Has he taught you the basics, and have you practiced them?"

"Yes," I replied, my voice barely audible.

"Alright, then. Think of either a number or a color. Hide it deep within your mind."

I closed my eyes, focusing intently. I erected mental barriers, brick walls, locked doors, and iron chains, determined to protect my secret.

"Ready?" Easton asked, his voice low and intense.

"Yeah," I replied, taking a deep breath. I could feel his mental presence probing my mind, a sensation both strange and unsettling. It was like someone was poking at my brain with a stick, inducing a wave of nausea.

After a moment, Easton spoke. "Purple."

My eyes flew open, shock spreading across my face. "How did you get past those barriers?" I demanded.

"You're not trying hard enough," he replied, a hint of frustration in his voice. "As soon as I started probing, you reacted, and your energy dissipated. You focused too much on the barriers, not on protecting your thoughts."

I was silent, disappointment weighing heavily on my heart.

"Again," he commanded.

We repeated the exercise, each attempt more frustrating than the last. By the tenth try, Easton was visibly agitated. "I can't do this right now," he snapped. "I need a break."

"I'm trying!" I pleaded, my voice rising.

Easton stepped closer, his anger palpable. "You're not trying hard enough!" he yelled.

"Hey, she's doing her best," Calix interjected, his voice sharp. "Stop being so hard on her!"

Sara chimed in, her voice filled with concern. "Yeah, stop yelling at her!"

Aiden exchanged a tense glance with Easton as if talking to him telepathically.

"You know, you've all been out here for a while," Easton began, his voice dripping with sarcasm. "And all she can do is shield herself from others' thoughts. Pretty useless in

Eternium, where everyone's trained to keep their minds closed."

I felt a wave of frustration wash over me. I was doing my best, but it wasn't enough.

Aiden stood up, his anger simmering. But before he could take a step, Easton was sent flying backward, crashing into a tree. A sharp intake of breath echoed through the forest as everyone's eyes widened in shock.

Sara rushed to Easton's side, concern etched on her face. Calix, on the other hand, couldn't contain his laughter. Aiden turned to me, his expression a mix of surprise and worry.

"Are you alright, my love?" he asked, his voice gentle.

"Yeah, why?" I replied, confused.

"You just used an ability you haven't even tried yet," he said, his voice filled with awe.

A sudden wave of dizziness washed over me. "I think... I think I need to sit down," I muttered, my vision blurring.

Calix, finally catching his breath, rushed over to assist Aiden and me.

"What did I do?" I asked, dazed and confused as they helped me sit down.

"Honey, what you did was hilarious!" Calix exclaimed, still chuckling.

Aiden smiled, his eyes filled with concern. "I'll tell you later. Calix, keep an eye on her."

"Sure thing," Calix replied, his gaze lingering on Aiden's ass as he walked away.

"You know he's taken, right?" I stated, playfully.

Calix chuckled. "Doesn't mean you can't admire the view."

As I sat there, I tried to piece together what had happened. The memory of the incident was fuzzy, a hazy blur. I hadn't physically pushed Easton, that much I was sure of. So what had happened?

"Calix, what exactly happened back there?" I asked, my voice filled with confusion. "Did I... did I do that?"

"Yeah, he really got under your skin," Calix mused, his eyes narrowing. "You don't remember, do you?"

I pressed my hands to my temples, a throbbing headache beginning to form. "No," I mumbled.

"Here, eat this," Calix said, handing me a protein bar. He rummaged through his bag, pulling out a bottle of water and a packet of aspirin. "When he was criticizing you and Aiden, the air around you started to shift. Aiden and I noticed it, but Easton was too caught up in himself. You were manipulating the air, drawing energy from it. It was like you were calling on a power you didn't even know you had."

"I didn't mean to..." I whispered, feeling a wave of guilt wash over me.

"Don't worry, sweetie," Calix reassured me. "Everyone knows it wasn't intentional. You were just defending yourself." He patted my shoulder. "You're doing great, Ember."

His pep talk did little to ease my guilt. I was worried about Easton, and I dreaded facing Sara. Her reaction was sure to be... colorful.

Aiden returned, a mischievous grin playing on his lips. "He's fine. Sara took him for a walk to calm him down. But he won't be walking very far for a while..." He chuckled.

Calix joined in the laughter. "That's great!"

"But how did I do that?" I asked, still baffled.

"It's a part of your abilities, my love," Aiden explained, his expression turning serious. "When you were overwhelmed, something else took control."

"What do you mean?" I asked, growing increasingly alarmed.

"You weren't possessed," Aiden chuckled, trying to lighten the mood. "Don't worry, you'll be fine. This is just a new challenge for us to overcome. Maybe it's a skill from a past life, something you unlocked in a moment of intense emotion."

I was bewildered. I understood his explanation, but it still felt surreal.

"Man, it must be tough being inside your head," Calix remarked, his eyes filled with empathy. "Aiden and I had to relive our past lives, but you're constantly reliving everything like it's happening for the first time. Talk about bad luck. And you're always asking questions, always wanting to understand. I wouldn't want to be in your shoes."

His words stung, though I knew he didn't mean to be hurtful. It was just Calix being Calix. Aiden, sensing my discomfort, pulled me closer.

"Learning new things and asking questions isn't bad, my love," Aiden reassured me, his fingers gently tilting my chin. "It might seem frustrating, but at least you don't have to relive every detail of your past lives, the good and the bad." His face remained impassive, but a flicker of sadness crossed his eyes.

"Remembering everything isn't always a blessing."

"I can imagine," I replied, understanding the weight of his words. "At least you have Calix. He understands you, truly understands you."

Aiden offered a bittersweet smile.

"Ok lovebirds, I need something to eat. If you are willing to wait for the broken asshole to return, be my guest." Calix broke out before walking away with his sword unsheathed, leaving Aiden and me alone.

With Calix gone, an unusual silence fell between Aiden and me. It had been a while since we'd had a moment alone, uninterrupted by training or threats. The awkwardness was palpable, at least for me. Aiden, however, seemed perfectly at ease. Instead of focusing on my abilities, we simply talked and laughed, enjoying the simple pleasure of each other's company.

Aiden opened up to me, sharing stories of his childhood with Calix and the confusion he felt when his past lives began to surface. He spoke of the relief he found in Calix's understanding. Then, his gaze turned to me, and his voice softened. He shared intimate details of his dreams, his memories of us together. As he drew closer, his words became more tender, his touch more gentle. But just as our moment was reaching its peak, Sara and Easton returned.

Easton limped towards us, his expression a mix of pain and annoyance. Broodingly and forcefully, Easton began speaking, "It has come to my attention that I was being too hard on you Ember."

Aiden couldn't resist a sarcastic remark. "What gave it away?"

The tension between the two men was apparent. It was clear that their rivalry, though subdued, still simmered beneath the surface.

Easton shot him a piercing look before speaking, "If you wish to continue, which I highly recommend, I will be resting in my tent. Come on, Sara." Sara obediently followed him, and they vanished from sight.

"How long have you been friends with Sara?"

I exhaled deeply as I thought. "I've known her since I was around five or six years old."

"Wow... I wish I had a friend for that long."

"Yeah... I can understand that in this life. We haven't been spending much time together lately. She mostly just follows Easton around."

"She might say the same about you." Aiden teased.

"Not quite. I don't hide my boyfriend and abandon her to spend time with him. I'm not upset with her now, but she tends to focus on one person."

After spending a few hours wandering through the dense woods, we decided it was time to return to camp. But before heading back, we thought it wise to check on Easton. After all, he had taken a bit of a tumble. And perhaps, we could squeeze in a bit more training.

Easton lay sprawled on the ground, his gaze fixed on the flickering flames. Sara sat beside him, a concerned look on her face. As we approached, Easton glanced up, his expression a mix of annoyance and resignation.

"I've been thinking," I began, awkwardly. "Perhaps we should continue training."

"Alright," Easton replied, his tone flat. "But I think I'm better suited to teach you something else. Aiden can handle the mental gymnastics."

Aiden smirked. "Afraid she might hurt you again?" he taunted.

Easton's eyes narrowed. "No. My methods just aren't working."

"Enough," I interrupted, growing impatient. "Let's just get on with it."

"Ember, sit in front of me," Easton instructed, his voice low. "Aiden, you can sit opposite Sara, but keep your distance from Ember. You don't want to distract her."

Aiden raised an eyebrow. "You're going to teach her..."

"Yes," Easton confirmed, cutting him off.

"Are you sure this is a good idea?" Aiden asked, his tone skeptical.

"It's time," Easton replied, his voice hardening. "Especially if you two aren't going to trust me."

I sat down, a wave of apprehension washing over me. "What are you going to teach me?" I asked, my voice barely a whisper.

"I'm going to teach you how to unlock someone's mind," Easton replied, his eyes glinting with a dangerous light. "Someone like me, someone like Lucien."

Fear gripped my heart. What if he pushed me too far? What if I hurt him again? What if I killed him? Sara would never forgive me, even if it was an accident.

Reading my hesitation, Easton responded, "This won't take much instruction.

You won't get emotional. Don't worry, you won't hurt me physically."

"Great, so I just have to worry about giving you a mental handicap," I muttered sarcastically.

Easton chuckled. "No, it's not like that. You'll just be unlocking memories, painful memories for both of us. But you have to break through those barriers."

I nodded, a sense of dread washing over me. I imagined Easton's frustration as I struggled to grasp the concept.

"Alright," Easton said, his voice low. "Now, focus on the silence, the mental barrier you feel around me." He paused, his gaze intense. "Do you feel it?"

I nodded, my concentration unwavering.

"Now, you need to enter a meditative state. Everyone, be quiet. Don't disturb her."

Frustration threatened to consume me, but I took a deep breath, focusing my energy on breaking through. Slowly, the barrier began to weaken, crumbling under the relentless assault of my will. As I delved deeper, the world around me faded away, replaced by a swirling vortex of thoughts and emotions. The wind stilled, and the world hushed. I was alone, adrift in a sea of consciousness.

Determined, I pushed forward, seeking the heart of Easton's mind. But as I ventured deeper, I realized the vastness of his thoughts, a chaotic labyrinth of memories and desires. It was like wandering through an endless library, each book filled with a different story.

Disappointment washed over me. Had I reached the limit of my ability? Was this all there was to it? Just a jumbled mess of thoughts and feelings? I opened my eyes, ready to admit defeat. But then, something shifted. A new path appeared, a hidden corridor leading deeper into the labyrinth. Curiosity piqued, I followed the path, eager to uncover the secrets it held.

A formidable barrier loomed before me, its strength far surpassing the previous one. What secrets lay beyond this wall? With renewed determination, I pushed against it, my will a tangible force. The barrier shattered; a silent explosion that echoed through the ethereal landscape.

I found myself in a dimly lit room, a cacophony of voices filling the air. Figures moved with a blur-like speed, their conversations a blur of words and emotions. I could see Aiden and Easton, young and carefree, discussing matters of little consequence. It was a mundane memory, a snapshot of a lifelong past.

I continued my exploration, traversing through countless memory fragments, each one more inconsequential than the last. It seemed Easton had carefully crafted this mental labyrinth, burying the true treasures deep within.

Then, I saw it: a peculiar door, standing alone in the middle of a vast, empty field. The door was battered and worn as if someone had desperately tried to force their way through. Intrigued, I approached the mysterious portal.

Beyond the battered door, a world of secrets awaited. Excitement pulsed through me, tempered by a growing sense of dread.

This was the heart of the matter, the core of Easton's memories.

The door creaked open, revealing a dimly lit room. The air was cold and still, the silence broken only by the echoes of distant voices. A scene unfolded before me, a memory brought to life. Easton stood before a grand desk, Lucien's imposing figure looming over him.

"What have you learned about the girl this time?" Lucien's voice, cold and commanding, filled the room.

"Not much, sir," Easton replied, his voice filled with apprehension. "She keeps her distance, wary of my intentions."

Lucien grunted in frustration. "That's usually what attracts her to you."

"Perhaps there's another way to gain her trust," Easton suggested his voice barely a whisper. "She cares deeply for her friend."

"Go back out there and don't return empty-handed," Lucien ordered.

The scene shifted, the focus narrowing onto a furious Lucien confronting a terrified Easton. "You are to leave Sara alone and return here! We already know Ember isn't going anywhere!"

"But it would be better if I stayed," Easton pleaded. "I could keep an eye on Aiden."

"Don't worry about him," Lucien dismissed. "I have him right where I want him."

Easton's face fell. "The girl will get in the way. I've gathered more information from Sara than I have from Ember."

"You've wasted too much time with her," Lucien scolded. "Focus on Ember."

"That's because Ember runs away whenever she sees me," Easton explained. "I've gathered more information from Sara. Her mind is a treasure trove of memories and thoughts, a goldmine of secrets."

Lucien scoffed. "Unimpressive. I already know where to find her, and I'll send my soldiers to collect her when the time is right."

He stood, his gaze piercing Easton's. "You think you've found your soulmate?" he asked, his voice dripping with contempt.

"No," Easton replied, his voice devoid of emotion.

"Good," Lucien sneered. "Then you should have no problem breaking things off with her. People thinking they have soulmates... how pathetic."

The room was a testament to neglect, dust motes dancing in the stagnant air. Lucien sat slumped in his chair, his face obscured by a shadowed hand. Years seemed to have etched themselves onto his features, his once vibrant spirit now a mere flicker. A half-read book lay forgotten on the desk before him, a stark contrast to his idle mind.

Easton entered the room, his presence barely acknowledged by the brooding figure behind the desk. A weight seemed to hang heavy on his shoulders, his mind preoccupied with thoughts unknown.

A long moment passed, the silence broken only by the ticking of a distant clock. Then, Lucien's voice, raspy and weary, cut through the stillness. "It's time for you to return to Terrah."

Easton's face was a mask of shock. "Why the sudden change of plans?" he asked.

"It's nearly time for Ember's powers to fully bloom," Lucien replied, his eyes fixed on the book in his hand. "We need more information on her, any new abilities she may have shared with Sara or others."

"Yes, sir," Easton replied, a flicker of excitement in his eyes as he turned to leave.

"One more thing," Lucien added, his voice barely audible. "Present her with the locket."

Easton nodded and disappeared from the room.

The remaining memories were largely inconsequential, routine reports and mundane tasks. Easton returned to Terrah, gathering information on Ember and her companions. But then, a more recent memory surfaced, a chilling reminder of Lucien's true intentions.

"If you can't find Ember or that meddlesome Aiden, we'll have to use Sara," Lucien growled, his voice filled with menace. "She'll be our leverage."

Easton's expression turned grim. He knew what Lucien was planning, and he feared for Sara's safety.

Easton's expression turned grave. "What do you mean, sir?" he asked, his voice barely a whisper.

"We'll give her a reason to come here," Lucien replied, a sinister smile playing on his lips. "If Sara is in danger, she'll come running."

Easton remained silent, his mind racing.

"Is there a problem?" Lucien asked, his tone sharp.

"Of course not, sir," Easton replied, his voice carefully controlled. "But how can you be sure Ember will fall for it?"

"She will," Lucien assured him, his confidence unwavering. "And that meddlesome Aiden will get in the way. She's so predictable."

A wave of disgust washed over me as I watched the scene unfold. I wanted to escape this horrifying vision, but I was trapped. How could I break free from this mental prison?

Chapter Fifteen

Easton's Secrets

The room stretched out before me, a desolate expanse. A single, imposing door stood in the distance, its chains rusted and broken. This was a different kind of challenge, a physical barrier rather than a mental one. Frustration gnawed at me as I approached the door. *How long would this test last? Would I be trapped here forever? Is Easton forcing me to stay?*

With a surge of determination, I focused my energy on the door. The chains snapped, the heavy metal groaning in protest. The door creaked open, revealing a dimly lit room.

A scene unfolded before me, a stark contrast to the previous visions. A young Easton stood in the shadow of Aiden, his jealousy clear. Aiden, the golden boy, the king's favorite, seemed to effortlessly excel at everything. As Lucien's influence grew, so too did Easton's resentment.

The scene shifted, revealing a more sinister plot. Easton, consumed by envy and desperation, followed Aiden on a secret mission to Terrah. A mission to find a mysterious girl, a key to unlocking Lucien's desires.

A devious smile crept across Easton's face as a plan began to form in his mind. He would undermine Aiden and tarnish his reputation.

"Sir, I have evidence that Aiden is hiding Ember and has been intentionally sharing information about you and our realm," Easton announced, his voice dripping with malice.

Lucien's eyes narrowed, his anger evident. "Bring them to me," he commanded.

Easton bowed and left the room, a sinister glint in his eye. He gathered a group of loyal followers, ready to carry out his plan. Their target: Aiden and Ember.

I watched in horror as Aiden was subjected to relentless torture. Tears streamed down my face, my cries echoing through the silent void. Easton, a shadow of his former self, stood by, a twisted satisfaction glinting in his eyes. Lucien, the puppet master, praised his loyal servant. A deep-seated hatred for Easton consumed me, a burning desire for revenge.

I was trapped, a prisoner in Easton's mind. My previous self, helpless and alone, was locked away, unable to aid Aiden in his time of need. Lucien, in his cruelty, had ensured that I remained oblivious to Aiden's suffering.

One day, a chilling scene unfolded before me. Lucien dragged my former self into the courtyard, where Aiden was chained to a post, his body battered and bruised. Aiden's eyes lit up with hope when he saw me, but that hope quickly turned to despair as he realized my helplessness.

The sight of Aiden's suffering was almost too much to bear. His once vibrant spirit was now broken, his body a testament to Lucien's cruelty.

Lucien's voice echoed through the courtyard, his words dripping with venom. "Aiden, you stand before us, a traitor. Your arrogance and defiance have sealed your fate."

He paused, his gaze fixed on Aiden, "You could have been great, a true servant of the realm. But your loyalty lies elsewhere."

Aiden, battered and bruised, met Lucien's gaze with defiant eyes. "Nothing you could offer could ever outweigh the bonds of true friendship and love," he spat.

Lucien's face contorted with rage. "Kill him," he commanded, his voice cold and emotionless.

As the guards moved to carry out Lucien's orders, a wave of despair washed over me. I was powerless to intervene, a mere spectator to Aiden's suffering. The scene was a stark reminder of Lucien's cruelty and Easton's betrayal.

At that moment, I understood the depths of Lucien's depravity. He was a master manipulator, a puppet master pulling the strings of fate. And I, a pawn in his grand game, was destined to suffer.

My former self struggled against the guards, her cries reverberating in the courtyard. "No! Aiden!" she pleaded, her voice filled with desperation.

Easton hesitated a flicker of remorse crossing his face. But then, he obeyed Lucien's command.

"Kill him!" Lucien ordered again, his voice cold and calculating.

I watched in horror as the guards moved to carry out the order. My screams filled the air, a desperate plea for mercy. Lucien's laughter echoed, a chilling sound that sent shivers down my spine. "Now, my plans will come to fruition," he declared.

Easton, a shadow of his former self, watched the scene unfold, a sense of guilt gnawing at his conscience. I, too, was a prisoner, confined to my room, subjected to endless tests and trials. Lucien's disappointment was more than apparent, his frustration evident in every interaction.

Days later, chaos erupted within the castle. Easton, his face etched with a mixture of anger and desperation, stormed through the halls. Lucien, disturbed by the commotion, emerged from his chambers, his voice laced with irritation.

"What is all this noise? Can't you people do anything right?" he demanded, his eyes scanning the room.

The room fell silent, a heavy tension filling the air. No one dared to move or speak, their hearts pounding in their chests.

"Easton, what is going on?" Lucien demanded, his voice laced with anger.

Easton looked at his comrades quizzically. "I would, but I have no idea, sir."

Lucien stormed towards the room where I was imprisoned. The door stood open, the room empty. A cold dread settled over him. A loud crash echoed through the hall, followed by a blood-curdling scream.

Easton rushed into the room, his heart pounding. There, on the cold, hard floor, lay my lifeless body, surrounded by shattered fragments of my soul. I had taken my own life, a desperate act of defiance against Lucien's tyranny.

A wave of despair washed over Lucien. His grand plans, his eternal reign, had been thwarted by a single act of defiance. As he stared at my lifeless form, he knew that he had failed.

A tapestry of horrors unfolded before me, a grim procession of lifetimes, each more tragic than the last. In every era, the same pattern repeated: Easton, the reluctant villain, driven by a twisted fate. Again and again, he found me, his actions fueled by a desperate hope, a misguided loyalty. Each time, he betrayed Aiden, a friend turned foe, a sacrifice on the altar of Lucien's ambitions.

With each betrayal, a new layer of guilt was added to Easton's burden. He was a puppet on a string, dancing to a tune he didn't understand. The ultimate goal, the reason for his actions, remained shrouded in mystery. Was it power? Immortality? Or something far more sinister?

The weight of these visions grew unbearable. The endless cycle of pain and suffering was too much to bear. I yearned to escape, to break free from this torment. But how could I when I was trapped within the depths of another's mind?

Frantically, I searched for an escape, a way to silence the echoes of the past. Closing my eyes, I took deep breaths, trying to calm my racing heart. When I opened them, I found myself in a different place and time.

It was graduation day, a bittersweet moment captured in a memory. I watched as Easton, a young and hopeful man, gazed at Sara with longing. A familiar story, a familiar pain. I knew the outcome, the bittersweet ending that awaited them.

He watched her from afar, a silent observer, torn between his love for her and his duty to Lucien. The desire to embrace her, to hold her close, was overwhelming. But he knew the consequences of such an act.

Easton couldn't afford to let Lucien know he'd found his soulmate. Such a weakness would be exploited. Lucien, ever suspicious, had zero tolerance for his soldiers forming attachments. Easton needed to maintain his position, his every action calculated and controlled. But now, their secret exposed, they were all in danger. Lucien, with his keen eye and uncanny ability to sniff out deceit, would undoubtedly discover their hidden connection. Every word, every action, every moment of vulnerability, could potentially betray them.

My eyes snapped open, the world blurring into focus. I was back, but something felt different. The others stared at me, their expressions a mix of shock and concern.

"How long was I in there?" I asked, my voice trembling.

"A few minutes," Aiden replied, his voice filled with uncertainty.

"It felt like days," I muttered, wiping away the tears that had silently fallen.

"That's because of all the information you had to process," Easton explained, his voice flat.

I glanced at him, a sense of pity washing over me. Despite his flaws, he was a prisoner of his own fate.

"Now you know everything," Easton said, his gaze fixed on the fire.

Aiden met my gaze, his eyes filled with a silent question. "Can we leave?" I asked, my voice devoid of emotion.

The weight of the world seemed to rest on my shoulders as I struggled to comprehend the horrors I had witnessed.

Aiden nodded, and together, we walked towards the camp. "Goodnight, Ember!" Sara called out, her voice a distant echo. I barely acknowledged her, lost in the fog of my own thoughts.

The fading light cast long, eerie shadows across the forest floor. A chilling silence enveloped the night, broken only by the occasional rustle of leaves or the distant cry of a nocturnal creature. Aiden and I walked side-by-side, our footsteps muffled by the soft earth.

"So, what did you find out about our '*pal*'?" Aiden questioned.

I let out a long sigh. "You two have a very complex relationship."

Aiden's eyebrows furrowed, his curiosity piqued.

"It's easier to understand his feelings for Sara than it is when it comes to you," I replied.

Aiden's eyes narrowed. "Could you be more specific?"

"He saw you as a friend, a rival, perhaps. But when you surpassed him, his jealousy turned to envy. The opportunity to strike you down, to eliminate the threat you posed, was too tempting to resist."

Aiden's anger flared. "I'll show him what it means to lose everything," he vowed, his voice filled with rage as he turned to walk back toward Easton.

I grabbed him by his arm. "Aiden, don't. There is enough guilt in him to torment him for several lifetimes."

Aiden hesitated, his expression conflicted. He knew I was right, but his anger still burned bright.

"Easton's going through a lot right now," I said, my voice filled with empathy. "He's hiding Sara from Lucien, and he's haunted by his past actions. More importantly, he's hurting, more than you can imagine."

Aiden remained unmoved.

"Let's just go back to the tent before you do something rash," I pleaded.

He nodded before we started our way back to camp.

****

On the way back, Aiden was in a playful mood. He teased me, jumped out at me from behind trees, and even chased me through the woods. I couldn't help but laugh, enjoying this lighter side of him.

When we reached the campsite, we found Calix fast asleep next to the campfire. We tiptoed past him, trying not to disturb his peaceful slumber.

"He must've been having one hell of a dream to be kicking and whining like a dog," I said to Aiden when we were safely in our tent.

Aiden smiled, his eyes sparkling. Something about his expression made my heart flutter.

"What is it?" I asked nervously

He leaned in, his breath warm against my skin. "You're so beautiful," he murmured, his eyes burning with desire.

My lips trembled as I smiled.

A shiver ran down my spine as his gaze held mine captive. His touch was gentle, his lips soft. As he deepened the kiss, a surge of electricity coursed through me. His hands, strong and sure, traced the curves of my body, igniting a fire within me as his fingers played at my shirt.

My hands slowly wandered up his shirt, tracing his abs in response. A quick break from our kiss to remove his shirt, before he deepened our lock, causing my core to tremble.

His fingers grazed my skin, sending shivers down my spine, my skin to form goosebumps. Slowly, methodically, he peeled away my shirt before cupping my ass, picking me up to him. I instinctively wrapped my legs around his waist, feeling his bulge grow, and my excitement intensified.

Aiden gently laid me down on the sleeping bags. He straddled over me at first taking in the sight of me before tenderly kissing me. My tongue tasted his deliciously sweet mouth and my heart started to race fast. His hand wandered from my breasts to the rim of my pants, undoing the button and zipper. His hand slowly found its way under my panties, causing my heat to melt. A moan escaped my lips from his electrifying touch as he continued caressing my core.

His excitement grew hard against my thigh. My hands instinctively moved to unbutton his pants, to set his growing bulge free. Aiden suddenly broke away, leaving both of us breathless, with lust in his eyes. Despite his desire, he was trying to show restraint, a mix of longing and reluctance evident on his face.

"Make love to me," my raspy voice stated before Aiden could say anything.

He studied me as I continued unbuttoning his pants, causing me to blush. Under his watchful gaze, I became embarrassed and a little self-conscious. I have never been so bare in front of anyone.

Aiden smiled softly before kissing my neck, stirring a soft moan to escape from within me, and his rod to twitch.

Hovering over me, my fingers played in Aiden's hair as his mushroom stood at my entrance. Giving me a deep, passionate kiss, he slowly thrust himself inside. A wave of ecstasy washed over me, a sensation so intense it took my breath away. Each touch, each movement, ignited a fire within me. His lips moved against mine, a dance of passion and desire. My body arched against his, a silent plea for more. As he explored my body, I felt a surge of pleasure, a sensation so intense it was almost overwhelming.

Aiden's eyes darkened with desire as he felt my response. He groaned, his body trembling with pleasure. With each thrust, I clung to him tighter, my nails digging into his back as I moaned his name.

An hour later, we collapsed into each other, wrapped up in each other's arms. When I finally caught my breath, I looked up at Aiden, a soft smile playing on my lips.

He placed his hand on the side of my face and caressed my cheek. "I love you."

"I love you too," I replied, giving him a long, lingering kiss before turning over on my side to get comfy. My butt brushed up against him and I could feel him harden again. "Really?" I asked amused as I sat up to look at him.

"Yeah... don't pay any mind to that." He said with an unforgiving smirk. "I can't help the way you make me feel."

I turned my body towards him, kissing his neck. Slowly, reaching down to grasp his rod.

Aiden pulled away, his eyes still closed. His breath was ragged, his voice a mere whisper. "Baby," he groaned, "you don't have to... You need rest." His words were fragmented, his thoughts clouded the desire fueled by my touch.

Ignoring his words, I moved to straddle him.

"We don't have to–" He began again, gripping my love handles.

"I want to," I stated, grabbing his member and moving him closer to my core.

His hands moved up my curves as I slowly began riding him.

"Ember..." he moaned.

Chapter Sixteen

Birthday

A week had passed since the unsettling encounter with Easton's mind and I found myself avoiding him at all costs. It wasn't an intentional reaction, but I found myself staring at him with pitying eyes. Yet I couldn't shake the feeling of his complex internal turmoil.

Sara, sensing my discomfort, had grown increasingly concerned. She'd peppered me with questions about Easton, his thoughts, his feelings. But I'd remained silent, unwilling to share the dark secrets I'd uncovered. It wasn't my place to judge him, nor was it mine to reveal his innermost thoughts.

To escape the growing tension, I retreated to my tent, seeking solace in solitude. The forest, once a place of wonder and adventure, now felt claustrophobic. I focused on controlling my abilities, shielding my mind from the intrusive thoughts of others. It was a delicate balance, a constant struggle to maintain my sanity.

Aiden, noticing my withdrawal, sat beside me in the tent. "Ember, what's wrong?" he asked gently, his voice filled with concern.

I remained silent, my eyes closed, lost in thought. "Nothing," I murmured, my voice barely audible. "I'm just practicing."

"You know I can see right through you," he replied, his tone firm. "What's really bothering you?"

"Seeing inside Easton's mind has changed everything," I confessed, my voice heavy with emotion. "It's hard to see him the same way."

Aiden nodded understandingly. "I understand," he said, his voice soothing. "But you can't let it consume you."

"I know," I replied with aggravation. "It's just... Sara only cares about how Easton sees her. She's so caught up in their own little world."

Aiden listened patiently, his expression thoughtful.

I let out a sigh, my thoughts a tangled mess. I focused on my training, desperate to regain control of my emotions.

"You're not mad at me, are you?" Aiden asked, his voice filled with concern.

"Why would I be?" I replied, my heart sinking. I couldn't bear the thought of hurting him.

"You've been keeping to yourself lately," he observed. "Especially since we..." giving a knowing smile.

I blushed, the memory of our intimate moment flooding my mind. "It's not you," I kissed him for more assurance before closing my eyes to focus on my prior objective.

Aiden hesitated before continuing, "Ember... You need more practice breaking into people's minds if you are going to defeat Lucien."

My eyes snapped open, a surge of adrenaline coursing through me. "What do you mean?" I demanded, my voice sharp.

"You'll have to infiltrate his mind, and steal information without his knowledge," Aiden explained, his tone grave.

"I thought you said I wouldn't be near him!" I exclaimed, anger bubbling within me.

Aiden's eyes softened. "I will protect you, I promise," he reassured me. "But you're the only one who can truly defeat Lucien. I can only do so much."

"If Easton is telling the truth if he's truly on our side, then we have a chance," Aiden said, his voice filled with hope. "But we need to be careful. Lucien is always watching, always scheming."

My heart sank. Aiden's words echoed in my mind, a stark contrast to his previous promises.

"I haven't lied to you, Ember," Aiden assured me, his voice gentle. "There's something bigger at play, a chance to strike back at Lucien."

His words offered little comfort. The weight of the world seemed to rest on my shoulders. I had been so focused on my own fears and doubts that I had failed to see the bigger picture. Perhaps it was time to embrace the chaos, to embrace the unknown. After all, what did I have to lose?

Anger fueled my training over the next few days, a dark fire burning within me. I sparred relentlessly with Calix during the day, my movements sharp and precise. Yet, a growing sense of unease lingered. I avoided Sara and Easton, their presence a constant reminder of her insecurities and his other complexities.

As I sat in my tent at night, lost in thought, Aiden joined me. "Ember, we need to train you to break into minds," he said, his voice serious.

I stared at him, disbelief etched on my face. "I don't want to do that again. It's so *wrong*."

Aiden sighed. "I know, but it's necessary. It's the only way to defeat Lucien."

"Whose mind am I supposed to break into?" I asked, rolling my eyes.

"Mine," Aiden replied, a mischievous glint in his eye.

"You?" I exclaimed, incredulous. "Now that definitely feels wrong."

Aiden smiled, a knowing look in his eyes. "Just try it," he urged.

Closing my eyes, I focused on Aiden's mind, attempting to penetrate the barrier. It was far more formidable than Easton's, a fortress of thoughts and emotions. I struggled, pushing against the invisible wall, but it held firm.

When I finally opened my eyes, Aiden was staring at me, a smirk playing on his lips. There was something almost challenging in his gaze, a spark of amusement.

Closing my eyes again, I renewed my focus. I would break through that barrier, no matter what. I probed his mind, searching for a weakness, a vulnerability. But Aiden's defenses were impenetrable, a true fortress.

Frustration began to gnaw at me. How could someone be so guarded? Was there a hidden technique, a secret trick to bypass his defenses? As I pondered the puzzle, I realized that the key might lie not in force, but in subtlety. Perhaps a gentle nudge, a subtle suggestion, could open a crack in his defenses.

I'd exhausted every technique I knew. Perhaps a more forceful approach was needed. I imagined my probing to be that of a sledgehammer, a blunt instrument of destruction, and a pickaxe, sharp and precise. With renewed determination, I focused my energy, channeling it into these mental tools.

The barrier wavered, then shattered, like glass breaking under a heavy blow. I was pulled into a swirling vortex, a maelstrom of thoughts and emotions. I was lost, adrift in the depths of Aiden's mind.

I plummeted through the darkness, an eternity passing in the blink of an eye. Finally, with a jarring thud, I landed on the cold, hard floor.

Pain shot through my body as I struggled to sit up. The room was pitch black, silent, and oppressive, amplifying my fear.

Panic began to set in. How long would I be trapped here? Lost in the labyrinth of Aiden's mind. I was alone, utterly and completely alone. My heart pounded in my chest, and my breath was short and shallow. The darkness seemed to close in around me, threatening to consume me whole.

Just as despair began to overwhelm me, a sudden tug pulled me forward. I was being dragged, helpless, through the darkness.

Suddenly, I was back in the tent, Aiden was closer to me, his hands on my face with his concerned gaze fixed on me. "Ember! Baby, everything is ok! Calm down, take a deep breath."

I blinked, disoriented. I had been so lost in the darkness that the fear and panic had spilled into the real world.

Calix rushed in with a cup of water and said, "Drink this."

My trembling hands reached for the cup, knowing it would help but fearing I would choke.

Aiden pulled me into a gentle embrace, his warmth soothing my frayed nerves. His lips brushed against mine, a long tender kiss that calmed my racing heart. Slowly, my breathing returned to normal, the panic fading away.

"Are you feeling better now?" Aiden asked, his voice soft.

I nodded, my heart still pounding. A lump in my throat obstructed my speech.

Calix offered me the water again, and I drank it greedily as if I hadn't had a sip in days. After several more glasses, my racing heart began to slow, and the fog in my mind started to clear. Exhaustion washed over me, and I felt a heavy weight pulling me towards sleep.

Reading my body language, Aiden suggested I rest. I nodded gratefully, collapsing onto the makeshift bed. As I drifted off to sleep, I couldn't shake the feeling of unease.

Later that night, I woke to the sound of Aiden entering the tent.

"Why is your mind so different from Easton's?" I asked, rubbing the sleep from my eyes. "His was so... chaotic."

Aiden smiled knowingly. "That's how I protect myself. Few can breach the first defense and if they do, they don't make it past the second."

"Then why did you want me to try?" I questioned, still puzzled.

"I wanted you to see the difference," he explained.

"Easton's mind is a labyrinth, full of secrets and hidden depths. There were only doors and invisible barriers... But yours... After breaking in, it was like I fell into a trap never to escape again..."

"And how hard was it for you to break through them?" Aiden challenged.

"Not too hard... It only took me a few tries." I admitted.

"Exactly," Aiden replied, his voice laced with a hint of concern. "If someone as inexperienced as you could break through, imagine what Lucien could do."

I pondered his words. "Those doors were pretty damaged. It seems someone has been there before."

Aiden shrugged. "He probably made it harder than it seemed. You're stronger now, more capable."

I stared at him, unconvinced. "I doubt it."

Aiden smiled, his expression reassuring. "So, what do you want to do? I know you're not tired."

"Tell me about our past lives," I suggested, curious about the countless lifetimes we'd shared.

Aiden hesitated, a flicker of apprehension in his eyes. "Are you sure?" he asked, his voice filled with uncertainty.

"Yes, please," I insisted. "It'll help pass the time."

Aiden sighed, resigned. "Alright," he said, settling down beside me.

I leaned forward in anticipation.

"You already know how we met the first time and how it ended through Easton's eyes. So, I'll start with our second encounter. We went to the same school when we were thirteen, just friends at first. But even then, I knew you were my soulmate, and of course, you felt that pull too. You were struggling with your abilities, lost and alone. I was the only one who could help you, the only one who understood, so naturally we grew closer.

"By the time we were fifteen, we were inseparable, lovers. But Lucien's shadow loomed large, threatening to steal you away. You were having nightmares, premonitions of the darkness to come.

"When we were twenty, we married, and Lucien's pursuit intensified. One day, his men found us, breaching our defenses. While I fought to protect you, you were taken captive. I watched helplessly as you disappeared."

Aiden paused, a shadow crossing his face. The pain of that day was still fresh, a wound that had yet to heal. My heart broke from the pain he was reliving.

"The next time I found you, my mother and I had just moved into town when we were 16. But this time, Lucien had one of his minions following you…

"It wasn't Easton. It was another one of Lucien's lackeys. After I dealt with him, Lucien's army attacked our school. A brutal battle ensued, and many lives were lost in our defense. We put up a good fight against so many and succeeded. But only three days later, Easton took you, right from our bed.

"The fourth time we met, it was in Victorian England. Calix, you, and I were inseparable, living a simple, happy life. But the shadow of Lucien loomed large. We knew it was only a matter of time before he found us. And he did. When you were just fourteen, he decided to take you…"

Aiden's voice trailed off, a distant look in his eyes. "I failed to protect you," he murmured, his voice filled with regret. "You slipped through my fingers."

Staring at me with guilt-filled eyes, I remained silent as he continued.

"The next time, I convinced myself that I was the reason Lucien kept finding you. I thought that if I distanced myself if I let fate take its course, you might be spared. I watched you from afar, a silent observer, while you faced the challenges of life alone. It was the hardest thing I've ever done, but I believed it was for your own good." Pain filled his eyes, "It was the dumbest decision I had made. It was only easier and more scary for you without me there.

"The next memory, you already know about from the dream in the forest. You already know how that ended, but as to how we met, we were sixteen. In that life, you had a very difficult time and were ready to just leave everything and everyone behind. I encouraged this decision and we traveled until you were ready to settle down. It took Lucien over a year to find us before…"

"The last time we met, I told you everything. Then, one night, Lucien manipulated you, convincing you that he could harm me; killing everyone you love. You, believing every word, went to him. Aiden finished, his voice filled with a mixture of pain and anger.

I knew there was more to the story, a darker, more sinister truth. But I also knew that he was struggling to relive those painful memories. I kissed his forehead, a gesture of comfort. "It's okay," I whispered. "You don't have to tell me everything."

Aiden's eyes met mine, a flicker of despair in his gaze. "Every time, you died. Whether by his hand or your own, the outcome was always the same. It haunts me, Ember. It haunts me."

My voice grew sad, "I'm sorry…"

Aiden glanced at his watch. "Happy birthday, my love," he said, a soft smile playing on his lips.

My eyes widened in surprise. "It's my birthday?" I exclaimed.

"It's midnight," he confirmed.

A wave of unease washed over me. I knew what this meant, a new cycle.

Just then, Calix burst into the tent, his face lit up with excitement. "Happy birthday, Ember!" he exclaimed, his enthusiasm infectious.

Aiden and I couldn't help but laugh at his over-the-top greeting.

Suddenly, a commotion erupted outside the tent. We rushed out to investigate, only to find Easton and Sara running towards us, their faces etched with fear.

"What's going on?" Aiden asked, his voice filled with concern.

"They found us! They're coming!" Easton's voice rang in my mind.

Aiden's voice, sharp and urgent, cut through the chaos. "Get inside, now!" he commanded. Without hesitation, I retreated to the tent, a wave of fear washing over me.

From the safety of the tent, I could hear the distant clash of swords and the panicked cries of the wounded. The flashes of light, like lightning in the night, illuminated the darkness outside. The sounds of battle grew louder, and more intense until they were abruptly silenced.

I pressed my hands over my ears, trying to block out the horrific sounds. But the echoes of pain and suffering persisted, haunting my mind. Suddenly, a wave of dizziness washed over me, and I collapsed to the ground. The last thing I saw was Lucien's sinister smile, his eyes filled with malicious intent.

****

I awoke with a start, my heart pounding in my chest. The tent was empty, the silence broken only by the distant sounds of chaos. A wave of dread washed over me as I remembered the chilling image of Lucien.

I rushed outside, my breath catching in my throat. The once peaceful campsite was now a scene of carnage. Bodies lay scattered across the ground, their lifeless forms a stark reminder of the violence that had unfolded. Easton, Aiden, and Calix stood amidst the chaos, their dirtied and blood-stained faces etched with anger and sorrow.

Easton's gaze fell upon me, his eyes filled with accusation. The silent judgment in his eyes was almost unbearable.

"It's all Ember's fault! She allowed Lucien into her mind! She is so pathetically weak!" Easton hissed, venom dripping from his words.

"No, Easton. It was your responsibility to ensure she was safe. You should have told her to hide somewhere!" Aiden retorted, his voice sharp and accusatory.

"What are you all arguing about now?" I demanded, irritation lacing my tone. "Where is Sara?"

Calix draped his arm on my shoulder, "Sara is gone," replied, his voice heavy with concern.

My heart dropped at Calix's words.

"We need to leave," Aiden declared, shooting a reproachful gaze toward Easton, "It isn't safe here anymore."

Easton's anger flaring, denied the accusation. "I would never endanger Sara! I didn't reveal our location to Lucien!"

"You'd sacrifice her to save yourself. Lucien wouldn't harm her, you know it. It's Ember he wants." Aiden's voice was ice-cold as he gathered his belongings.

"How dare you!" Easton sputtered.

"Enough!" I roared, my anger boiling over. "Easton quit blaming others for your reckless choices. What's done is done, get over it. There's nothing we can do to change it. Aiden, you just need to stop talking to him altogether. Calix, stop fanning the flames!"

Silence fell over the men. They feared my wrath, my uncontrolled power. My heart burned with frustration. Our secret was exposed, a failure likely caused by my own carelessness. Surrounded by clashing egos, I yearned for peace and understanding.

Chapter Seventeen

Lucien's Return

Days bled into one another, a monotonous march through the verdant obstacles. We four, a silent quartet, navigated the treacherous terrain, our words as scarce as water in a desert. Only the primal needs of rest and sustenance broke the oppressive silence. The tranquility, however, was a fragile illusion, shattered by Easton's petulant complaints. He railed against our endless wandering, demanding a return to the familiar, a place where the only struggle was against our own limitations. Aiden and Calix, weary of his ceaseless whining, retorted with biting sarcasm, reducing him to a child with their scornful words.

As the fourth night descended, a heavy cloak of fatigue settled upon us. Exhausted and irritable from their bickering, I told them it was time to rest. They nodded, their movements mechanical, and began the task of establishing camp. We had left behind the dense forest, venturing through diverse landscapes. We had traversed verdant woodlands, forded a rushing river, skirted the edge of a serene lake, and crossed a barren field. Now, we found ourselves in a less oppressive wood, a place where the trees stood apart, inviting the sunlight to dance upon the forest floor. We made camp beside a gentle river, its soothing murmur a lullaby to the weary soul.

As soon as my eyes closed, I was plunged into the desolate cityscape, a hauntingly familiar nightmare. Yet, this time, fear was absent, replaced by a burning rage. I strode through the desolate streets, a defiant figure, my heart filled with anger. Many questions clawed at my mind and I demanded the answers. I will confront the monster and force the truth from him.

"Lucien!" I bellowed, my voice echoing through the silent streets. "Show yourself, coward! I will no longer be a pawn in your twisted game!"

A swirling vortex of darkness materialized before me, coalescing into a humanoid form. Lucien, cloaked in shadows, emerged, his lips curling into a sinister smile as he savored my defiance. "Do you truly believe you have a choice?" he taunted, his voice a chilling whisper.

I glared at him, my anger a tangible force, yet I was shackled by the knowledge of his power. He was the puppet master, pulling the strings of this twisted reality. Any attempt to strike back would be futile, a mere ripple against the tide of his dominion.

"Do you truly believe you have the upper hand?" I retorted, my voice laced with defiance.

"In this realm, I am omnipotent," he proclaimed, his voice dripping with arrogance. "I can weave your reality, inflict unimaginable suffering upon those you cherish, and extinguish your life with a thought."

"Then do it," I challenged, my voice unwavering. "What's stopping you? Oh, that's right, you need me."

"Indeed," he drawled, a sinister glint in his eye. "It is a cruel irony that I must rely on one such as you. I could, of course, extinguish your life, wait for your return, and begin this torturous cycle again. However, I have grown weary of such games. So, for now, you will serve my purpose."

"What have you done with Sara?" I demanded, my voice edged with desperation.

He sneered. "You humans, always so self-sacrificial. You worry for others while your own doom approaches."

"Oh, really? You, the paragon of selflessness? The man who's always thought of others before himself?" I scoffed, my voice dripping with sarcasm. "Why don't you enlighten me with some groundbreaking revelation I haven't already heard? Something truly shocking, like the sky being blue or water being wet."

"Don't presume to know me, Ember. As I've said, compassion is a weakness, a foolish indulgence. There's no greater folly than caring for another soul."

"Is that so? Perhaps you should consider that caring can also be a source of strength. A quality you, unfortunately, seem to lack."

The cloaked figure lunged, a beast unleashed. A guttural roar escaped his lips, a sound born of pure, unadulterated rage. Yet, I stood unmoved, my gaze unwavering. His fury, though intimidating, failed to ignite fear within me.

"Sara," I demanded, my voice steady, "Where is she?"

He halted, inches from my face, his breath hot and heavy. A flicker of surprise danced in his eyes, a testament to my unexpected defiance.

"Locked away in my prisons," he hissed, his tone icy.

"Why her?" I pressed.

A wicked grin split his face, revealing a predatory gleam in his eyes. "A mere pawn in a grand game," he sneered, his voice dripping with malice. "A tool to bend you to my will." He turned away, his words echoing in the silence. "What better way to make you beg than to strike at your heart?"

"Why not Aiden?" I questioned, my voice laced with curiosity.

"A banished fool, unable to return," he scoffed, his tone dripping with disdain. "And a reckless one at that. He'd only cause chaos."

I couldn't suppress a chuckle. "So, you're afraid of him, is that it?"

Lucien lunged, his fist connecting with my jaw. I tumbled to the ground, pain shooting through my face. He stood over me, his eyes burning with a cruel satisfaction. "Don't you dare suggest I could fear such a pathetic creature! He's nothing but a bug, easily crushed. I've done it twice already!"

Rage ignited within me. "He's more than that to you! More than you could ever be!"

A smirk twisted his lips. "I can make him suffer simply by taking you from him."

"I would love to see you try!" I struggled to my feet, my jaw throbbing. "You think you won? You have already come and left without me."

"You'll do anything to save her, won't you? You'll surrender, you'll obey. I have you exactly where I want you, Ember."

"Oh, you think you've got it all figured out, do you?" I scoffed.

"Why wouldn't I?" he replied, his voice dripping with arrogance.

"What if I decide not to play your little game? What if I let Sara suffer the consequences?"

He burst into laughter. "Please. You wouldn't dare. You're too loyal, too selfless. You'll do anything to save her."

Confusion clouded my mind. "What if I choose not to? What if I simply refuse to give in to your demands."

A sinister grin spread across his face. "No, Ember. You're trying to fight fate. You're the key to a much larger puzzle. And you, my dear, are trapped."

"Destiny? Fate? I don't buy into that. I make my own choices, not some cosmic force."

Lucien's laughter echoed through the room. "Belief doesn't matter. Fate has its own plans."

"Fortune cookie nonsense, more like it," I retorted, rolling my eyes.

His laughter ceased, replaced by a more serious tone. "Then what do you think will happen?"

Ignoring his question, I shifted the focus. "The faceless man in my dreams. What happened to him? Did you kill him, or is he going to make an appearance?"

His expression turned to one of pure anger. "How dare you speak to me like that!" he roared.

Victory was mine as I laughed, reveling in his discomfort. "The king stripped you of your powers, making you vulnerable. So, you resort to intimidation tactics, sending faceless men to torment me. How sad and pathetic. You speak of the weakness of soulmates, yet you rely on your followers for everything. I can't fathom why anyone would follow or fear you. You're powerless."

Enraged, Lucien lashed out, his hand connecting with my face, sending me crashing into the wall. He advanced, his grip tightening around my throat. "You know nothing of my reign, the old king, or my true power! Everything you know is tainted by Aiden's lies."

Gasping for air, I managed to croak out, "I also know who you truly are from Easton's mind."

Lucien released me, a flicker of fear and excitement flashing across his face. "You've grown stronger," he muttered, more to himself than to me.

I clutched my throat, trying to regain my breath. "I will never use my powers to help you."

He turned to face me, his eyes burning with intensity. "Oh, you will. Whether you like it or not."

Before I could respond, I was jolted awake by Aiden's concerned voice.

"My love, are you alright? Wake up!"

I groaned, sitting up slowly. A throbbing pain pulsed through my head. "I'm fine," I muttered, annoyed at the interruption.

Aiden examined me closely, his eyes scanning the tenderness of my neck and body for injuries. "What did Lucien want?" he asked, his voice filled with concern.

"Just his usual intimidation tactics," I replied, dismissing the incident.

"But what did he say?" he pressed, his voice growing stern.

"He has Sara and knows I'm stronger now. As always, he wants me to do his bidding," I explained, my tone flat.

Easton stormed into the tent, "And what possessed you to tell Lucien about reading my mind?" his voice filled with anger. "Do you have any idea how reckless that was? You've put us both in danger!"

"Could you keep it down?" I snapped, my head throbbing. "I've got a headache, thanks to *your* king."

"I don't care what he did to you! If he hurts Sara because of your stupidity, you'll have me to answer to!" Easton roared.

"And what exactly are you going to do?" Aiden challenged, standing up. "Do you think you can get through Calix and me?"

"It's been done before," Easton growled, stepping closer to Aiden.

"Enough, both of you!" I intervened, stepping between them. "Easton, he's not worried about you. The only thing he is worried about is how *powerful* I have become. So don't get your panties in a bunch, he isn't worried about you or Sara." This information took him by surprise. "And he knows I won't abandon Sara, but I don't know how I can sneak in and out without alerting him."

"You're not going," Aiden declared.

"Why not?" I demanded, my voice laced with anger and disbelief.

"Because you're not ready," Aiden replied, his tone firm.

"She needs to go to him, Aiden," Easton insisted. "There's no other way."

"If you're so concerned about your soulmate, why don't you go save her?" Aiden retorted. "No one would suspect you."

"Lucien has guards watching her 24/7," Easton explained. "And he'd immediately suspect me of helping her escape."

"Easton, you need to leave," Aiden said firmly. "Ember's had enough for one night. She doesn't need your reckless ideas."

I didn't respond, my mind racing.

Easton gave me a longing look before exiting the tent.

"Why did you make him leave?" I asked Aiden, frustration growing. "I'm going to Eternium, whether I'm ready or not."

"You're not going until you're ready," he replied coldly, turning to leave the tent.

I didn't call out to him, nor did I argue. I knew what I had to do, but one question lingered: Could I leave knowing Aiden disapproved? The answer was clear. I couldn't bear to disappoint him. It would only bring back painful memories of times I'd recklessly rushed to Eternium. I couldn't inflict that pain on him again.

Chapter Eighteen

Checkmate

Knowing Lucien was the creature from my nightmares, a strange mix of pity and disdain washed over me. While I didn't condone his actions or understand his need for power, I no longer feared him. His threats, once so terrifying, now seemed hollow. All this training, all this preparation, for a man who couldn't physically harm me? It felt absurd. He was a broken shell, a man who'd lost too much and clung desperately to what remained. Desperation could fuel determination, but Lucien lacked that spark. Yet, even as pity stirred within me, there was something about him that remained enigmatic, a puzzle piece missing.

The following day, I sat by the riverbank, watching the water flow calmly. Suddenly, the tranquility was shattered by the familiar sounds of Easton, Aiden, and Calix arguing once more.

"We have to rescue Sara!" Easton insisted, his voice filled with urgency.

"And I've told you, Ember isn't ready!" Aiden retorted, his tone firm. "This conversation is over." With that, he turned and walked away.

Calix, clearly frustrated, followed suit, hoping to escape the tension.

The silence that followed was peaceful, but it was soon interrupted by the sound of approaching footsteps. It was Easton, his face etched with worry and frustration. He sat down beside me, his shoulders slumped.

Ember, you agree that we need to get Sara right?" Easton asked.

"You know I do," I responded.

"Then why don't you talk some sense into Aiden?"

"You think you're the only one having trouble convincing him? He won't even let me get a word in edgewise," I argued.

Easton let out an exasperated sigh. "What if I sneak you off to Eternium? Aiden would never know."

"Right, except for when I'm missing for days, and so are you. Easton, you know he'd think you betrayed him. No, we have to convince him to let me go."

"By then it may be too late!" Easton insisted, his voice filled with desperation.

"Lucien himself told me he won't harm Sara. He only wants me," I replied, trying to ease Easton's worries.

Easton stood up, his frustration evident. He hurled a rock into the river and stormed off into the distance.

I stayed by the river, lost in thought, for another hour. When I was sure Aiden had calmed down, I stood up and stretched. I began searching for him, eventually finding him and Calix sparring deep in the woods. My heart pounded in my chest as I approached them, nerves getting the better of me. But before I could chicken out, Aiden spotted me and walked over, concerned.

"What's wrong, my love?" he asked, his voice filled with worry.

"Nothing... I just wanted to talk, but if you're busy, we can do it later," I replied shyly.

"We can talk now," Aiden said with a smile. He turned to Calix, signaling that we were leaving.

The sun was high in the cloudless sky as we walked through the forest. Spring had arrived, painting the landscape with vibrant colors. The trees were adorned with lush green leaves and delicate pink blossoms. A carpet of wildflowers blanketed the forest floor, and fresh green grass was beginning to emerge. Birdsong filled the air, a harmonious symphony of nature. The atmosphere was charged with energy, yet the scene was serene and peaceful.

Aiden and I strolled through the woods, sharing laughter and lighthearted conversation. It was a welcome respite from the constant stress and worry. But the moment of peace was short-lived.

"So, what did you want to talk about?" Aiden asked, his voice cutting through the tranquility.

My heart pounded in my chest. I hesitated, unsure of how to broach the sensitive topic. "I wanted to talk to you about Lucien..." I mumbled nervously.

"Ember, I told you I didn't want to discuss it any further," Aiden replied, his tone firm.

"I'm not trying to upset you," I said, looking down at my feet. "It's just something we need to discuss, even if you put your foot down, it can't be helped."

Aiden stared at me, his expression unreadable.

"Why are you being so stubborn? You knew this was coming! You even told me I'd have to go to Eternium without you!" I argued.

He turned away from me. "I only said that to push you. It might have annoyed you, but it helped you gain more control over your abilities."

"So you weren't planning on letting me go?" I asked, surprised.

"No. I swore to protect you. I know we're the only ones who can stop Lucien, but... I can't lose you again, my love," he admitted, turning back to face me.

"But he has my best friend," I replied. "I can't just leave her there. If I don't show up, he'll kill her."

"We'll find a way to rescue her," Aiden assured me.

"You know there's only one way," I countered.

"Ember, you're not ready to face him," he argued.

"I'm stronger than ever! You've said it yourself! Or was that a lie too?" Pain flashed across his face at my words. "I know how to protect myself from him, Aiden! Lucien is powerless. He has nothing to protect him."

"He has his own army and his telepathy," Aiden argued.

"There's too much at stake for him to kill me. You know he wouldn't, and he never has," I countered.

Aiden stared at me, unconvinced.

"What's the worst he's done to you? He's never physically harmed you," I pointed out.

"He may not kill you, Ember, but he would hurt you, physically and mentally. He's tormented you for years. If that's not proof enough, I don't know what is," Aiden insisted.

"I don't think so... Something tells me he wouldn't..." I replied, my voice wavering.

"And why is that? Besides him placing you in nightmares since you were a child and beating the shit out of you, what makes you think he wouldn't hurt you in reality?" Aiden asked, his voice laced with anger.

"I don't know. There's something about him that's hidden. I haven't been able to figure it out," I admitted, my voice wavering.

"That's not a good enough answer," Aiden replied, his tone firm.

"Aiden... do you trust me?" I asked, my voice filled with both seriousness and a hint of sadness.

"Of course I do, my love," Aiden replied, his fingers tracing the curve of my cheek. "But you must understand my perspective. For centuries, I've watched you be stolen away from me. Careless mistakes may have been the catalyst, but the outcome was always the same: your death. Sometimes it was swift, sometimes drawn out over days or even months. I don't know if you chose your own fate or if Lucien's cruelties forced your hand. How would you feel knowing that your beloved was doomed? What lengths would you go to prevent their inevitable demise?"

"I've lost you too," I replied, tears welling up in my eyes.

"You don't remember it firsthand. You only see it through my memories or those of others. You don't relive every moment, every emotion as if it just happened. You can't truly understand the depths of the pain, the fear, the despair. It's a weight that I carry alone, a burden that no one else can share. You can't comprehend the terror of losing you, of watching you slip away, knowing that I might never see you again. It's a darkness that consumes me, a void that nothing can fill. You simply can't understand."

My heart ached as tears threatened to spill over. I know I couldn't fully understand the depth of Aiden's pain, the agony of losing me over and over again. Yet, his words still cut deep. "Aiden," I began, my voice trembling, "you may have lied about facing Lucien, but that deception fueled my strength and courage. I no longer fear his cruelty; there's a deeper, more complex being beneath the surface. If I can get close to him, I might uncover his hidden vulnerabilities. It could be the key to reclaiming our lives, to restoring peace to Eternium."

Aiden's gaze fell to the ground as he contemplated my words. Finally, he looked back at me, a sigh escaping his lips. "You've made a compelling argument, my love," he admitted. "But it's not that simple. I'm sorry, but I don't see a good outcome from this."

I turned away, as I began to sob. "Then what was the point of all this? Taking me away from my family, hours of grueling physical and mental training—all for nothing? You're asking me to abandon my friend, to let her die at Lucien's hands. I can't do that."

"I know you couldn't, Ember," Aiden said, his voice filled with understanding. "I don't expect you to."

"So you expect me to just walk away from you?" I asked, turning to face him, showing the tears I tried to hide.

"No, but I do expect you to figure out a way to rescue your best friend," he replied flatly.

"Without your permission?" I questioned, my eyebrows raised.

"It depends," he said cryptically.

"But you know I wouldn't do that to you, especially after everything you've shared with me," I replied in a quiet tone.

Aiden didn't respond to my words. Instead, he offered a sad smile and a subtle nod before turning and walking away, lost in thought. As he retreated, he paused, casting a lingering glance over his shoulder. "I would bend the universe, defy the laws of physics, just to stay with you," he murmured, before leaving me by myself.

My heart felt heavy as if a lead weight had settled in my chest. Aiden's words echoed in my mind, a bittersweet reminder of his love and the sacrifices he was willing to make. I felt a pang of guilt and shame, knowing that I had caused him pain. The once-bright spring day now seemed bleak and dreary.

As I walked back to camp, I spotted Easton waiting for me.

"Not now, Easton," I said, my voice tinged with annoyance.

"Did you talk to him?" he pressed.

"You're really insufferable, you know that?" I retorted, more harshly than I intended. I knew I shouldn't have snapped at him, but Easton's persistence was getting on my nerves.

"Did you talk to him?" he asked again, undeterred.

"Yes, I asked him," I replied, my voice laced with irritation.

"And?"

"What do you think?" I retorted, glaring at him.

He stared at me, his face a mask of frustration. "This is so frustrating!" he exclaimed.

"I know," I replied, my voice soft. "But we need to be patient."

"No," he insisted, his voice rising. "I refuse to sit idly by while my soulmate is held captive. You're just twiddling your thumbs because you're afraid to disobey Aiden."

"How would you feel if Sara had been taken away from you not just once, but multiple times?" I demanded, my voice rising. "How would you feel if your best friend betrayed you, setting in motion a cycle of suffering that led to Sara's premature death in every lifetime? Wouldn't you cling to every moment, every hour, every minute with her before she was inevitably taken away? But you wouldn't understand that, would you?"

My words, fueled by frustration and despair, stung him. His face flushed with anger as he prepared to retaliate.

"Listen here, pal. I'd never let Sara out of my sight, and I wouldn't make the same boneheaded mistakes Aiden did. And if he wanted to spend every second with you, where is he now? Protecting you? No, he's not. I could snatch you up and take you to Eternium right now, and he wouldn't be able to do a damn thing about it!"

I stepped closer to Easton, my gaze intense. "Oh, you wouldn't make the same mistakes? And where's Sara right now? Huh?" I spat. "I dare you to take me to Lucien. But what about you? What would happen to you? I know more dirt on you than even Lucien does. And if Lucien doesn't get you, what do you think Aiden and Calix would do?" A sinister grin spread across my face as Easton's color drained. "Now, I suggest you leave before I make you. If I find a way to help Sara, I'll let you know. But for now, get lost!"

Easton stood there, stunned. Even I was surprised by my outburst. I didn't know where the sudden surge of anger had come from, but it felt cathartic. For a moment, the weight of frustration and helplessness seemed to lift.

Chapter Nineteen

Shattered

Later that evening, as the sun dipped below the horizon, painting the sky with hues of blue, yellow, orange, and finally, the inky blackness of night, a serene and romantic scene unfolded. A chorus of chirping birds and croaking frogs filled the air, signaling the end of another day. The four of us sat around a crackling campfire, their faces illuminated by the dancing flames. A comfortable silence hung in the air as we carefully considered the delicate topic that weighed heavily on our minds. Sara, a sensitive subject for both Easton and Aiden, was the elephant in the room. All eyes turned to Calix, the only one who hadn't yet voiced his opinion.

"So, Aiden," I began, my voice barely a whisper as I glanced nervously at my plate, "did you give any more thought to what we discussed earlier?" I couldn't bring myself to meet his gaze.

Aiden's response was curt. "Yes," he replied, his tone leaving no room for further discussion.

Shifting my attention to Calix, I pressed on. "Calix, I'm sure you know all about the argument dealing with Sara. What are your thoughts?"

He met my gaze, his eyes flickering with fear and resentment. It was clear he didn't want to be drawn into this, but I had to know. I hated putting people on the spot, but this situation demanded a solution, and I was dealing with two stubborn men.

"What do you mean?" he managed to say while choking on his food.

"Do you think I'm ready to go to Eternium?" I asked, my voice steady.

"Ember, don't drag him into this," Aiden interjected, his tone flat and dismissive.

"I want to hear his opinion," I insisted. "It's just his opinion. It won't change anything. You know that."

"Look, honey," Calix began, setting down his plate, "I think you could use a little more training. But I also don't understand why you're learning all this if you might never even go. It seems a bit pointless."

"So you're conflicted," I replied, my voice laced with irritation.

"Yeah... I mean, I don't trust Easton to protect you. As soon as Sara is free, I think he'll just disappear. No one would ever find him."

"Hey!" Easton protested, but his words were cut off by Calix and me.

"Shut up!" I snapped, my voice sharp and angry.

"Well, it's the truth!" Calix bit back.

"I know Aiden can't go to Eternium, but what keeps you from going?" I asked Calix curiously.

"I'm not from that plane of existence, so I can't simply travel between realms. I could potentially hitch a ride with Easton or someone else, but that's not an ideal solution. If you're suggesting I go to Eternium to rescue Sara, I'd be trapped there. If Easton were to leave, as I fear he might after Sara's release, I'd be stranded, with or without Sara. That would put you and Aiden back in the same predicament, trying to figure out how to get me back, a task only you could truly accomplish. And there's no guarantee I'd even survive the jump."

"But I'm not from that world. I can't travel between realms, but I did survive the jump," I stated.

"Actually," Easton interjected, his voice carrying a weight of revelation, "you do have the ability to travel between realms. You were originally from Eternium."

"What?" I stammered, disbelief coloring my voice.

"Long ago, King Aldrich's great-great-great-great-grandfather banished you to this world for your protection. You were special, destined for great things in our realm, blessed with extraordinary abilities. Unfortunately, most of these powers remain dormant. But they knew that if someone were to seize control of Eternium with a heart consumed by darkness, you could become a powerful weapon, a threat to the entire realm. From what I have gathered over the years, it is also told that you are a member of the royal family." Easton stated, his voice low and deliberate.

"You're full of crap," I scoffed, dismissing his claim outright. "There's no way that's true."

Aiden, however, seemed intrigued. "Actually," he mused, his eyes widening as he considered the possibility, "that makes perfect sense."

Calix remained frozen in shock, his expression a testament to the absurdity of the situation.

I was speechless. This couldn't be real. "How could any of this be possible? I wasn't even born there!" I exclaimed, struggling to reconcile this new information with my understanding of reality. Yet, a part of me, deep down, began to entertain the possibility. A strange sense of doubt crept in, questioning the limits of my own understanding.

"Originally, yes. But due to the circumstances of your banishment by a royal ancestor, you've been repeatedly reborn here," Easton explained. "Your family here is your biological family, but your true origin lies in Eternium."

"Okay, but if that's true," I pressed, still confused, "how is it that Aiden and I age and die, while you, Lucien, and everyone else from Eternium seem to stay the same age?"

"Time flows differently in our realm, a lot slower than here," Easton replied. "It is also helpful that our lifespans are significantly longer than those of humans in Terrah."

I was speechless. No matter how hard I tried to deny it, the pieces of the puzzle were falling into place. A strange sense of certainty washed over me, confirming the truth of Easton's words.

A heavy silence settled over us as we each processed the revelation. Our thoughts were abruptly interrupted by a rustling sound from the nearby bushes. We all jumped to our feet, our hearts pounding in our chests. The only sound was the gentle flow of water, making the sudden noise all the more unsettling.

Calix cautiously approached the bush.

"Maybe it's just an animal," I suggested, though I didn't fully believe it myself.

Aiden moved closer to me. "It's always better to be safe than sorry," he said.

Easton's voice was grave as he spoke. "They're here."

Twenty cloaked figures burst from the shadows, their sudden appearance startling us. As I tore my gaze away from the encroaching figures, I could faintly hear Easton's voice, but his lips remained motionless. A disembodied voice echoed through the air, repeating, "I'm so sorry, please forgive me. It had to be done."

My expression shifted from shock to a cold, accusing glare. "What did you do?" I demanded, my voice laced with anger and betrayal.

His eyes, filled with fear and sorrow, met mine. "I'm sorry," he whispered, his voice barely audible.

Aiden, ever the protector, moved towards Easton with a menacing stride. But I, consumed by a fiery rage, was no longer the damsel in distress. A power, long dormant, stirred within me, demanding to be unleashed.

A sudden gust of wind whipped around me, my hair swirling and dancing. Easton, paralyzed by fear, began to levitate. Aiden halted in his tracks, his gaze fixed on me in awe. With a flick of my wrist, Easton was hurled into the darkness, disappearing into the depths of the forest.

Calix, a whirlwind of steel and fury, danced with death, his sword a blur as it parried and struck. Aiden, a swift arrow of vengeance, loosed his deadly missiles, each one a harbinger of doom. I, a tempest of celestial power, hovered above the fray, a silent guardian, a force unseen.

A group of followers, emboldened by their numbers, converged upon Aiden, their weapons raised high. But before they could strike, I unleashed a torrent of icy wind, freezing them in place, their menacing forms encased in crystalline prisons. Turning my attention to Calix, I summoned a sphere of radiant energy, hurling it at the assailants who threatened his life. The orb exploded upon impact, a dazzling display of power that sent the enemies reeling.

From the shadows and the trees, a legion of cloaked figures emerged, their forms flickering into existence like phantoms. Aiden, his quiver depleted, was forced to rely on his bare fists and the agility of a wildcat. Calix, a whirlwind of steel and fury, danced a deadly ballet with his sword, each strike a testament to his skill and ferocity. Yet, even their combined might began to falter, their breaths ragged, their movements labored. The relentless onslaught of the enemy threatened to overwhelm them, each passing moment a test of their endurance and will.

As I battled with the relentless onslaught of foes, a flicker of movement caught my peripheral vision. A cloaked figure, dagger raised, lunged toward Aiden. I barely had time to register the threat before my ally reacted. With speed and precision honed by countless battles, Aiden parried the deadly strike, seizing the attacker's wrist and twisting it with brutal force. The dagger clattered to the forest floor as Aiden, with a swift and decisive motion, disarmed his opponent and turned the weapon against him. The tables had turned, and the once-threatening assailant was now at the mercy of Aiden's lethal counterattack.

This once tranquil haven had been transformed into a hellish battlefield, all because of Easton's betrayal. Aiden's warnings once dismissed as paranoia, now echoed with chilling accuracy. As my mind raced, desperately searching for any justification for Easton's actions, my powers began to falter. A searing pain, a relentless tide of agony, pulsed through my head, threatening to consume me. My knees buckled, and I collapsed to the forest floor, my body drained as I tried to stay conscious.

My vision blurred as I struggled to my feet, my body heavy and unresponsive. In the distance, I saw Aiden and Calix, locked in a desperate struggle with the relentless tide of enemies. They were too far away to hear my cries for help, and any attempt to call out would only distract them, putting their lives in further danger. My powers, once a beacon of hope, had dimmed, their light extinguished by the strain of overuse. I couldn't even muster the strength to send a telepathic message to Aiden, indicative of the extent of my exhaustion. I had pushed myself beyond my limits, and now I was paying the price.

I was helpless, a mere spectator to the brutal dance of life and death. Time seemed to stretch and warp, each agonizing second an eternity as I watched my soulmate and friend fight for their survival. Calix, his arm a crimson river, bore the mark of a deep, grievous wound. His head, a canvas of bruises, bore witness to the relentless assault. Yet, he persisted, his spirit unbroken, his determination unwavering. Aiden, too, was battered and bloodied, fought with a savage intensity, each strike a desperate plea for respite.

Just as a glimmer of hope flickered, a new wave of assailants emerged from the shadows, their numbers seemingly endless. Aiden and Calix, their strength waning, their bodies battered and bruised, fought on with desperate resolve. Their clothes, once pristine, were now tattered and stained with blood and dirt. Their weapons, once sharp and deadly, were dulled and chipped from countless clashes. As the battle raged on, they were forced to scavenge for new weapons, claiming them from the fallen foes. With every passing moment, their situation grew more dire, their survival hanging by a thread.

A piercing, agonizing noise erupted within my skull, accompanied by a deafening rush that threatened to drown out all other sounds. The pain was so intense, so unexpected, that it rendered me speechless. My breath caught in my throat as a cold sweat broke out across my brow. I curled into a fetal position, my hands clamped over my ears, my eyes squeezed shut, desperately seeking refuge from the torment. Then, as suddenly as it had begun, the noise and the pain ceased, leaving me trembling and disoriented.

As I lay there, a flicker of strength began to return to my weary body. With a surge of determination, I pushed myself to my feet.

And then, he was there, standing before me. Easton. My heart pounded in my chest, a mix of shock and fear washing over me.

"I'm sorry, Ember. This is the only way." Easton said, his voice filled with regret.

Before I could react, he grabbed my arm, his grip firm and unrelenting. My body, weakened by the ordeal, was no match for his strength. As I struggled against his hold, a desperate cry escaped my lips. "Aiden!" I screamed, my voice echoing through the forest. My hand outstretched, I reached for my soulmate, my eyes pleading for his help. His head snapped to see Easton holding me.

Immediately understanding the situation, Aiden rushed to me. His hand almost brushed against mine…

When there was nothing, but darkness.

Continue the story! Follow Ember, Easton, Aiden, and Calix to Eternium in Eternal Lament!

Eternal Lament (Book 2)

Trapped in the icy grip of the sinister Lord Lucien, Ember finds herself a captive in his opulent, yet chilling, Eternium. Betrayed by her closest friend, Easton, she's forced to play a dangerous game of deception, pretending to be a willing participant in Lucien's twisted plans. Ember must unravel the mysteries of her past, master her hidden powers, and rescue her kidnapped friend, Sara.

Meanwhile, Aiden, consumed by anger and despair, embarks on a perilous quest to save Ember. Alongside his loyal companion, Calix, he seeks the help of a mysterious figure who may hold the key to Eternium. But as fate intervenes, an unexpected ally emerges, offering a glimmer of hope.

With time running out and the fate of Eternium hanging in the balance, Ember must navigate a labyrinth of deceit, danger, and forbidden love. Can she outsmart Lucien, break the chains of darkness, and reclaim her destiny?

About the Author

Autumn Marie is a Louisiana-based writer and digital artist. Armed with a Bachelor's Degree in Digital Design and Animation, she blends creativity and technology to bring her stories to life. With a lifelong love of writing, she's excited to share her imaginative worlds with readers.